"*Me again,*" I typed. "*It's 11:55 on December 31st and I'm not at Seth Modine's party, wearing high heels and lavender lip gloss. 'Why, Lily Rebecca Walker,' you declare in astonishment. 'How could he have overlooked you when he made up his guest list?' Good question. I guess he just hasn't noticed me yet.*"

I stopped typing. My gaze wandered from the computer screen to the dark window. If Seth hasn't noticed me, I thought, then that makes him the only one. I'd always made it a point to be hard to miss. Whenever I change my style or my attitude or my friends, Mom says I'm going through a "phase." Once Rose called me a chameleon, but Laurel pointed out that I was the opposite—I don't change color to blend in with my environment, but to stand out from it. What a perfect Laurel comment—she always has to turn everything into an opportunity for nature education.

Now I tilted my head thoughtfully to one side. Maybe there are different ways of getting noticed, I mused. So, what do I have to do to get noticed the right way?

I went back to my journal. "*My big sisters make it seem easy,*" I wrote. "*Rose knows exactly who she is and what she wants to do in life, and so does Laurel, and so did Daisy. I wonder if now that I'm sixteen, I'll figure out who I am, too.*"

Don't miss any books in this dramatic new series:

THE YEAR
I TURNED
Sixteen

#1 Rose
#2 Daisy
#3 Laurel
#4 Lily

Available from ARCHWAY Paperbacks

THE YEAR I TURNED
I TURNED
Sixteen

LILY

Diane Schwemm

AN ARCHWAY PAPERBACK
Published by POCKET BOOKS
New York London Toronto Sydney Tokyo Singapore

AN ARCHWAY PAPERBACK *Original*

An Archway Paperback published by
POCKET BOOKS, a division of Simon & Schuster Inc.
1230 Avenue of the Americas, New York, NY 10020

Produced by 17th Street Productions, Inc.,
a division of Daniel Weiss Associates, Inc.
33 West 17th Street, New York, NY 10011

Copyright © 1999 by Daniel Weiss Associates, Inc., and
Diane Schwemm
Cover art copyright © 1999 by Daniel Weiss Associates, Inc.

ISBN: 0-671-00443-3

First Archway Paperback printing January 1999

10 9 8 7 6 5 4 3 2 1

AN ARCHWAY PAPERBACK and colophon are
registered trademarks of Simon & Schuster Inc.

Printed in the U.S.A.

IL 7+

For my grandmother,
Eunice Butler Schwemm

One

The day I turned sixteen was the most wonderful of my life! My devoted older sisters Rose and Laurel showered me with jewelry, gift certificates to the mall, and the complete works of Shakespeare in leather-bound volumes. As if that were not enough, my mom, the beautiful, recently remarried widow Maggie Walker, doubled my allowance and announced that from then on I wouldn't have chores or a curfew because I'd be going to boarding school in Paris."

"The end," I said out loud, scrawling the words at the bottom of the page. Then I slapped my notebook shut and tossed it on my desk. I had to laugh. "Yeah, right. I wish."

There couldn't be a worse time of year for my birthday: in between Christmas and New Year's, where it gets completely lost in the holiday shuffle. I get totally ripped off in the present department, or at least that's the way it *seems*, because people are always giving me "joint" Christmas and birthday gifts. But sixteen, I figured, is special. It had to be a big deal this year.

Throwing my bathrobe on over my nightgown—it was late morning, the day after Christmas, and I'd

1

slept in—I ran downstairs to see what everyone else was up to. Mom and Hal were in the kitchen, drinking coffee and looking at some papers spread out on the table. "Catering business stuff?" I asked.

Mom nodded at me, then turned back to my stepfather. "Hal, I've been thinking about overhead. Maybe we can cut it back if we . . ."

She leaned over to point something out to him. As her blond hair swung close to his face, he took the opportunity to kiss her cheek. Mom laughed, blushing. "Oh, Hal," she said, but she sounded pleased.

Rolling my eyes, I headed for the family room. Mom and Hal had just gotten back from their honeymoon a few weeks before Christmas, and you'd think they were twenty the way they were always gazing adoringly at each other and kissing in public. Mom looks great for her age, but she *is* in her forties, and Hal's at least fifty, and they've both been married before and have grown-up kids.

"The lovebirds?" Rose guessed when she saw my expression.

Rose and her husband, Stephen, and my other big sister, Laurel, were sitting on the couch with their coffee, watching the morning news. The room was still littered with scraps of wrapping paper and satin ribbon.

"Aren't they a little old for that?" I asked. "I mean, it's not like they just met. Mom's known Hal forever. They never *used* to act this way."

"Getting married is romantic," Stephen said,

slipping an arm around Rose's waist and pulling her close.

"Not you guys, too," I groaned as they smooched. "You've been married for a whole year and a half. Can't you show a little self-control?"

"I think Mom and Hal are cute," Laurel remarked as she pushed her unruly brown hair behind her ears. She clicked the remote control, switching to the public television channel and some boring nature show. Typical.

"Yeah, well, you don't have to live with them," I pointed out a little wistfully. I was the only sister still at home. Laurel's a freshman at the University of Maine—she's prevet. Rose is a singer and actress; she and Stephen settled in Boston after graduating from college. I'd had a third sister, Daisy—she was in between Rose and Laurel—but she was killed in a car crash when she was nineteen. "It's no fun at the dinner table lately, believe me. When they're not drooling over each other, they're talking about Mom's new store. I might as well be invisible."

Actually, this wasn't really true. Hal is a great guy and pays me a lot of attention. It was nice—having a father again, I mean.

"The store's a big deal, though," Rose said. She was now leaning against Stephen's propped-up knees so he could comb her long blond hair with his fingers. "Mom and Hal are investing a lot in it, and there's a ton of work to do beforehand."

My mom is a caterer. She started doing that to make a living after my father died eight years ago—his fishing boat was lost at sea in a sudden storm. At first it was tough for her to make ends meet, but now she's really successful—so successful, in fact, that she's going to open a gourmet food shop in town this summer. Hal's an accountant, and he's going to help manage the finances.

"I know it's a big deal," I said, nudging Laurel aside so I could sit, too. The show was about coral reefs, and there was a pretty hunky guy scuba diving with the tropical fish. "It's just a constant topic, you know? There are other important things happening these days."

"Like what?" Rose asked.

"*You* know," I said.

Rose wrinkled her forehead and turned to Stephen. "What do you think Lily's talking about?"

He shrugged. "Got me."

"I'm stumped," Laurel put in.

"I know. The after-Christmas sales at the mall," Rose guessed.

"You idiots!" I exclaimed. "Tomorrow's my birthday!"

"Your *birthday!*" Rose slapped the heel of her hand against her forehead. I caught her winking at Laurel. "I totally forgot. How old will you be? Fifteen?"

I knew she was pulling my leg, but I still got worked up. "*Sixteen*," I corrected indignantly.

"And it's tomorrow?" Laurel shook her head. "That doesn't leave much time to shop. Is it okay if I make the Christmas present I gave you, like, a joint present?"

"Absolutely not!" I declared. "Haven't you guys planned a party?"

"Ask Mom," Rose answered. "Stephen and I are planning to stick around for your birthday, but we need to leave late tomorrow afternoon. Remember I told you my agent, Carol, got me the audition with the touring company of a Broadway musical? I need to rehearse. Speaking of which . . ." She got to her feet and stretched her arms over her head. "Shower time."

Laurel stood up as well. "I have to leave tomorrow, too," she told me. "Do you think you could have your party in the morning?"

I scowled. "I'm not giving myself a party—you guys are supposed to do it!" Honestly. Didn't anyone care?

Rose finally took pity on me. "Don't worry, Lil. Mom's putting together a brunch, and we'll all be there with bells on."

"Brunch is perfect," Laurel said, heading for the door. "I'll call Carlos and tell him I'll be back in the afternoon."

"Your boyfriend's more important than my birthday?" I shouted after her, but she didn't answer. Which is just as well because obviously she would've said, "Yes." Duh, I thought. Carlos is a senior at U. Maine, and he's gorgeous. He and Laurel met years ago working at the local wild animal shelter, but they just started dating, and I couldn't exactly blame Laurel for wanting to hurry back to campus!

I trailed into the kitchen. Hal had disappeared, but Mom was still there. "Does brunch sound okay?" she asked, glancing up from her paperwork. "With just the family?"

"I *was* kind of hoping for a real party," I admitted. "Twenty or thirty people, semiformal attire, champagne punch . . ."

I wasn't kidding, but Mom laughed, anyway. "Oh, Lily," she said. "Your sisters' sixteenth-birthday celebrations were pretty low-key. That's our tradition."

"Well, I *guess* it's okay if it's just us," I said with a disappointed sniff. "Will there be a cake at least . . . with butter cream frosting?"

"Butter cream frosting," Mom assured me.

"Three layers?"

"Three layers."

I was satisfied. "All right. No joint presents, though," I told her.

Mom laughed again. "Heaven forbid!"

I ate breakfast and then went up to my room, which Laurel shares with me if Rose and Stephen are visiting. I changed into a high-waisted rayon dress and pinned my long, wavy blond hair up with the antique silver-and-garnet comb Rose and Stephen gave me for Christmas. I've always liked dressing up in funky, unusual clothes—lately I've been feeling kind of turn-of-the-century.

I went over to the window and looked out in time to see Laurel walking her dog, Snickers. People were going in and out of our building—we live on Main Street above Wissinger's Bakery, one of the busiest stores in our little southern Maine town, even in the winter, when it's just us locals. When I was really young, my family had a big beautiful old house on Lighthouse Road. It had been in the family for generations, but after Dad died, we had to sell it and move into town. Our apartment is nice, though, with three bedrooms on two floors. It feels like home to me now. Hal used to rent the apartment next door, but he moved in with us when he and Mom got married.

I stayed at the window, my eyes taking in the view. The Hawk Harbor marina was empty of all but fishing boats—the summer people's yachts were in dry dock—and beyond the marina the ocean was steel gray and choppy. I could see to the end of Rocky Point, where the country club is, and down the pine-covered coast a ways. In summer Hawk Harbor gets really crowded and busy. A lot of tourists vacation here, and fancy restaurants and boutiques have popped up all over the place—Mom's future store is a good example. Off-season, though, more than half the stores close and Hawk Harbor reverts back to being a small town. I like it that way. I love living in an old-fashioned place that's full of history and tradition.

I went over to my bookshelves, thinking I'd start reading one of the novels I'd gotten for Christmas. On the way I looked at two framed photographs on my desk.

I don't know anybody my age who's lost so many close relatives. One picture was of my father,

Jim Walker, who died when I was eight, and another was of my older sister Daisy, who died when I was fourteen. If she were still alive, Daisy'd be a junior at Dartmouth. She died right after Laurel's sixteenth birthday, and that autumn and winter were possibly the worst time of my life. Of all our lives.

Daisy was so special, I remembered, lifting the picture to study it more closely. In the photo she was holding a softball bat—her arms tanned and strong. Her blond hair was summer bleached, and her eyes sparkled with good humor. And Dad, I thought. I bit my lip. I hated to admit it, even to myself, but if it weren't for that picture on my desk, I might have forgotten what Dad looked like. It made me sad, but I couldn't help it. He'd been gone for half my life.

I was still holding the picture of Daisy, and now I studied it again. I have a whole album of photos of her, which I look through all the time, but for some reason this one means the most to me. It's just so *Daisy*. I don't like thinking about how her story ended—the rainy night, the car sliding off the slick road—so instead I cherish this single moment, Daisy and her softball bat, her beauty and strength preserved forever. She was so together— smart, athletic, popular, caring, independent, *genuine*. She'd been the backbone of our family after Dad was gone. She took care of me. She could fix anything. Anything at all.

In a weird way I felt closer to Daisy than ever

now that Rose and Laurel didn't live at home any-more and I was the only sister left. "I still miss you all the time," I whispered.

I kissed Daisy's picture, then carefully placed it back on the desk. I tried really hard not to think about the fact that my favorite sister hadn't lived to see me turn sixteen.

Mom's the best caterer in the state of Maine. Brunch the next morning was delicious and elegant: eggs Benedict, a basket of fresh-baked muffins, fruit salad, a cake on a pedestal, candles, good china.

At the end of the meal Rose said, "I bet Lily's ready for her presents. That's always *my* favorite part, anyway."

I blinked innocently. "There are presents for *moi?*"

"Yes, let's do presents before we cut the cake," Mom said.

Hal carried a pile of gift-wrapped boxes over to the table. There was a book from Laurel, a scarf from Rose and Stephen, and a video from Hal. "Um, not to seem greedy," I said to Mom, "but I was expecting something . . . else."

"Of course," she answered, smiling as she handed me a small velvet box. "I knew you were waiting for this."

I opened the box eagerly. On their sixteenth birthdays all my sisters had gotten gold charms from our great-grandmother's bracelet. What would mine be? I wondered.

"Oh, it's beautiful," I exclaimed when I saw the little gold book on a slender chain.

"You can open it up," Mom explained. "It's a locket."

I opened the locket. "I'll have to find a tiny, tiny picture to put in here. Thanks, Mom."

"Cake time!" Laurel said, hopping out of her chair. "I'll light the candles."

Everybody sang "Happy Birthday" and I blew out the candles. My wish, of course, was that someday I'd get to go to Paris. I felt as if I had everything else I could want.

As soon as brunch was over, Laurel, Rose, and Stephen had to rush around, packing stuff and tossing it into their cars. Mom handed them care packages of food, and then there was a flurry of hugs and kisses and they were gone.

Back to their real lives, I thought as I stood at the living room window, watching Rose and Stephen buzz off in the old Saab Stephen's been driving since high school.

I grew up in a big, lively family. Sometimes Rose, Laurel, and I get on each other's nerves, and sometimes I complain about being the youngest, but I like having my sisters around. Now my sixteenth birthday was over almost before it had begun.

I was an only child again.

On New Year's Eve day Noelle Armitage came over to listen to CDs and read beauty magazines with me. Noelle and I were neighbors when my family lived on Lighthouse Road, and we've been friends off and on forever. I'll admit that in sixth grade, I thought she wasn't cool and I started hanging out with some other girls. But in junior high we got close again. We both read a lot and love fashion. Noelle has excellent taste in clothes.

"What's with this?" Noelle asked, tossing a magazine my way. We were sitting on the floor of my room, our backs against the bed, a bag of pretzel sticks open between us. "Lavender lip gloss?"

"Easter egg colors are in. Look. *These* models have *yellow* lips."

"Maybe I should rethink my makeup for tonight. I was just going to wear *red* lipstick."

"Red's always acceptable," I assured her. "It's classic. And on New Year's Eve you want to look classic."

Stretching her arms over her head, Noelle let out a happy sigh. "Seth Modine."

I nodded. That was all there was to say. "Seth Modine," I agreed, somewhat grumpily.

Noelle had been invited to Seth Modine's New Year's Eve party and I hadn't. She didn't rub it in, and it wasn't like I was *devastated*, but it did bug me a little. Seth's part of the It crowd at South Regional High, and the fact that I wasn't on his guest list meant I wasn't. Not that I care about that sort of thing. Well, maybe I do—a little.

"Why did he invite you, anyway?" I asked Noelle. "I didn't even know you guys were friends."

"I think his bud, that Timothy guy, likes me. We're all in the same history class."

"Timothy Pratt? He's cute."

"He's okay." Noelle's pretty cute herself, with wide blue eyes and dead-straight, chin-length, pale blond hair.

Jumping up, she went over to my closet. "So, what can I borrow?"

I helped Noelle pick out a short, sexy black dress that I got as a hand-me-down from Rose. "What are *you* going to do tonight?" she asked.

"I don't know." I watched Noelle try on my shoes. I wasn't dating anyone special. "Mickey's going to a party at Daniel Levin's and she said I could go with her, but I can't get too excited about it."

Mickey is McKenna Clinton, another close girl-friend of mine. She's fun, but some of her other friends, like Daniel, are kind of quiet. "A party at Daniel's." Noelle laughed. "Isn't that an oxymoron or something?"

"Can you imagine Daniel busting a move on the dance floor?" I agreed.

Noelle shook her head and stuck out her right foot, modeling a black-beaded high heel. "Can I borrow these, too?"

"Sure," I said. "Someone might as well look hot tonight since I'll probably be sitting home, watching TV."

And that's what I ended up doing. Mom and Hal invited me to go with them to the annual New Year's Eve party at the Harrisons', but I couldn't picture myself there dateless. It was okay when I was a kid, but not now that I'm sixteen. I dressed up, anyway—I put on my Emily Dickinson gown and some fake pearl earrings, made microwave popcorn, and watched old Katharine Hepburn–Spencer Tracy movies on the family room TV.

Usually I'm as happy on my own as I am when I'm surrounded by people, but tonight, as the hands of the clock moved toward midnight and I had no one to kiss and wish Happy New Year, I felt kind of sad. The apartment, which had seemed so cramped when my family first moved in years ago, felt big and empty. The only people home, I thought, are me, myself, and I.

I didn't want to be lonely, not on New Year's Eve, so I turned on the secondhand laptop computer Hal gave me for my birthday last year and opened up a file called Journal.

"Me again," I typed. "It's 11:55 on December 31st and I'm not at Seth Modine's party wearing high heels and lavender lip gloss. 'Why, Lily Rebecca Walker,' you declare in astonishment. 'How could he have overlooked you when he made up his guest list?' Good question. I guess he just hasn't noticed me yet."

I stopped typing. My gaze wandered from the computer screen to the dark window. If Seth hasn't noticed me, I thought, then that makes him the only one. I'd always made it a point to be hard to miss. Whenever I change my style or my attitude or my friends, Mom says I'm going through a "phase." Once Rose called me a chameleon, but

Laurel pointed out that I was the opposite—I don't change color to blend in with my environment, but to stand out from it. What a perfect Laurel comment—she always has to turn everything into an opportunity for nature education.

Now I tilted my head thoughtfully to one side. Maybe there are different ways of getting noticed, I mused. So, what do I have to do to get noticed the right way?

I went back to my journal. *"My big sisters make it seem easy,"* I wrote. *"Rose knows exactly who she is and what she wants to do in life, and so does Laurel, and so did Daisy. I wonder if now that I'm sixteen, I'll figure out who I am, too."*

Just then the clock on the mantel struck twelve. "Happy New Year," I whispered to myself.

T w o

Second semester of junior year brought new classes and new teachers. Noelle and I were in first-period oceanography together, and before the bell rang, we slumped down in our back-row seats and whispered about Timothy Pratt. "He called the day after Seth's party and asked me out," Noelle confided.

"No kidding!"

"We're going to a movie this weekend."

"Wow!"

"I don't know, though." Noelle doodled with her mechanical pencil on the first page of a new narrow-ruled spiral notebook. We both love mechanical pencils and narrow-ruled paper. "I thought I had a crush on him, but now I'm not so sure. He gave me this quick kiss at midnight at the party and his lips felt kind of slimy."

I laughed. "He was drooling. Maybe you should be flattered."

Just then Mr. Hashimoto came in. Sitting down at his desk at the front of the room, he started taking attendance. He raced through the list pretty fast, but when he got to my name, which is always

15

one of the last ones, he looked up to study me over the rims of his gigantic rectangular-framed glasses. How come teachers always sport the most unfashionable eyewear? I wondered.

"Walker? Laurel's sister?" he asked.

"Yes," I replied.

"I had her in class last year. She was an outstanding student," he commented.

I just nodded. What was I supposed to say?

Noelle rolled her eyes. "Doesn't that drive you crazy?" she whispered.

"I'm used to it," I whispered back.

It was true. When you're the youngest of four kids who've all gone to the same schools, you hear that kind of thing all the time. For some reason, though, today it was worse than usual. First there was Mr. Hashimoto. Then in fourth-period English, Ms. Gates, who's been the drama adviser at South Regional for about a hundred years, went on and on about Rose. On my way into gym class I had to look at the pictures of Daisy with her sports teams and see the plaque dedicated to her. After class my gym teacher, Larry Wheeler, pulled me aside to reminisce about how great it had been coaching Daisy in softball and soccer, how she was the best athlete he'd ever seen at South Regional, and how he still missed her.

We spent a few minutes being sad together. "Everybody still misses her," I told him, a little choked up.

"She was extraordinary," Coach Wheeler replied, giving me a comforting pat on the back.

As I walked down the hall to my locker to grab a book for my last class, I had a weird sensation. I felt like a ghost.

I'm not Rose or Daisy or Laurel, I wanted to shout, so stop comparing me to them! But that was the problem. I'd tried on a lot of identities over the years but still hadn't found one that fit. I knew who I *wasn't*—my sisters—but I didn't know who I *was*.

I studied the other kids walking by me in the hall. Jock, I thought, mentally labeling each of them. Nerd. Bohemian. Cheerleader. Marching band. Everyone seemed to have a niche . . . everyone but me.

Mickey was waiting for me at my locker. "It's time to make my mark," I announced.

"What are you talking about?" she asked, flipping her long, frizzy brown braid over one shoulder.

We walked to class together, matching strides, while I tried to explain about feeling invisible, about not fitting in, about just being viewed as Rose and Laurel and Daisy's kid sister. "I'm always on the fringe of things. I feel like a lot of kids at school avoid me because they don't know what crowd I belong to. I'm too eclectic or something."

"That's what makes you unique," Mickey pointed out. "You have so many interests."

"I need *one* interest," I decided. "I have to start thinking about college, you know? My sisters all got scholarships. What makes *me* stand out? What am *I* good at?"

Opening the door to the stairwell, Mickey said,

"You're losing it, Lily. I really don't think you need to worry about this stuff." Mickey frowned a little. "Besides, it's not like you don't have friends. You have me and Noelle. Why do you need to be part of a crowd?"

I found myself picturing Daisy. She was my definition of success, and *she'd* had a crowd. "Maybe because it would help me figure out who I am," I explained. "And it's time. You know what my life's been like the last eight years, Mickey. We're in good shape now. Secure. *Normal.* My family makes sense again." I paused before adding, quietly, "Now I just need to make sense of myself."

The next week Mickey and Noelle came up to me in the hall after school one day. "Have I got something to show you," Mickey said as she grabbed my arm and hauled me down the corridor. Noelle strode after us. "Take a look at this," Mickey said.

She stood me in front of a poster on the wall outside the computer lab. I read it out loud. "'New creative-writing workshop . . . two days a week, one-half English credit for juniors and seniors . . . register with Mrs. Cobb by January fifteenth.'"

I looked at Mickey. "Why are you showing me this?"

"Are you kidding? It's perfect for you!" Mickey jabbed Noelle with her elbow. "Isn't it perfect for her?"

Noelle nodded, her white blond bangs bouncing. "Totally."

"I don't think so because—," I began.

"*This* is your identity. You have that stash of stories in your closet," Mickey interrupted. "You're *always* writing something."

"Yeah, but—"

"Let's go to Mrs. Cobb's office right now and sign you up," Noelle decided.

They tried to drag me off again, but I dug in my heels. "I don't think I want to sign up," I said.

"Doesn't it sound like fun?" Mickey asked. "I'm going to sign up."

"Yeah, but the thing with my writing is, I never show it to anyone," I reminded her. "Not even you guys. No way am I going to let a class full of total strangers read my stuff."

"It might not be total strangers," Noelle remarked. "Now that I think about it, I remember Timothy saying something about it. Something about *Seth* wanting to do it. I think we should all sign up. It would be cool to take a class like that together."

I went on shaking my head stubbornly. Seth or no Seth, I couldn't see it happening. Let other people read my stories? No way. "Come on, let's go. I feel like a burger at Cap'n Jack's."

We headed out to the parking lot and the baby blue VW Bug Noelle borrows from her brother sometimes. She likes to be seen in it because it matches her eyes *and* her retro Twiggy look. As we drove off to Cap'n Jack's, Mickey and Noelle started chatting about the movie we'd all seen last weekend in Kent. I didn't join in because I was still thinking about the creative-writing workshop. *It does sound interesting,* I thought as I looked out the car window at a brown, stubbly field bordered by skeleton-branched trees. *But I wasn't exaggerating when I said that I never show my stories to anyone.*

Writing was a private thing for me. *What would it be like to share it with the whole world?*

When Noelle dropped me off at home later, I found Mom in the kitchen, pureeing something pink in the food processor. "What are you making?" I asked, pouring myself a glass of seltzer.

"Roasted bell pepper and lobster bisque," she answered, "for the wedding lunch I'm catering this weekend. Would you toss me the pepper grinder, honey?"

I gave her the pepper grinder. "So, Mom," I said, pulling a stool up to the counter so I could nibble leftover cooked lobster. "I'm in this dilemma."

"What about?"

"Well, I'm a little bit good at a lot of things but not great at any one thing like Rose and Laurel are and like Daisy was," I concluded. "Daisy especially. How am I ever going to get a scholarship for college?"

"I know Hal and I have been talking a lot about finances lately," Mom said as she ladled hot broth into a big kettle, "about how we're putting all our eggs in one basket with the store. But I don't want you to think we can't afford to pitch in for your college tuition. You'll get financial aid, and we'll help you all we can."

"It's not just that," I said. "I need to *focus*."

"You have plenty of time to decide what you want to be when you grow up."

"But Daisy knew she wanted to be a doctor and—"

"Oops!" Mom jumped back as some broth splashed onto the range top. "Lily, would you throw me a dishcloth?"

I helped her clean up the spill. "I want to find my identity," I went on, even though Mom was too distracted to pay much attention. "There's this new creative-writing class at school, but . . . I just don't know."

"Well, you love clothes." She gave the broth a stir and stepped over to open the refrigerator. "How about fashion design?"

"I can't draw," I reminded her.

"I wouldn't worry about it if I were you," Mom concluded. "Something will strike you sooner or later. You're only sixteen."

Only sixteen, I thought as I clumped upstairs to my bedroom. Mom makes it sound like I'm still in kindergarten!

Later I took my laptop to bed and wrote in my journal for a few minutes before turning out the light. "*No one understands me these days. Mom thinks I should be perfectly content being the baby of the family forever. But I'm ready to grow up.*"

I stopped typing. Lifting my eyes from the keyboard, I met those of the blond girl in the photo on my desk. "What do *you* think, Daze?" I asked her. "I want to be famous but . . . at what?"

I remembered what Coach Wheeler had said the other day about Daisy. He'd called her "extraordinary." I shook my head, discouraged. Among the three of them my older sisters had done it all—there was nothing left for me.

I'm the baby of the family, I thought glumly, and I'll always just be ordinary.

Three

By lunchtime on Monday I had made my decision. I let Mickey and Noelle drag me to Mrs. Cobb's office to see if there were still openings in the new writing class. It hadn't started yet because it was just for partial credit, meeting twice a week, on Tuesdays and Thursdays during lunch period. "She wants to sign up for the creative-writing class," Noelle announced.

Mrs. Cobb looked at me, one salt-and-pepper eyebrow lifted. "Can she speak for herself?" she asked.

Noelle nodded. "Sure."

When I didn't speak, however, Mickey jabbed me with her elbow. "Um . . . ," I began.

"We're *all* taking the class," Noelle went on. "If there's still room for us."

"I can just squeeze you in," Mrs. Cobb replied. "Let me get your names."

Noelle and Mickey wrote their names on Mrs. Cobb's list. Then the pen was in my hand—the moment of truth.

I froze, my fingers clutching the pen. I stared at the sheet in a panic. I couldn't take this class. I couldn't let people read my stories. It would be like letting them see me naked!

Then I focused on a name at the top of the list. He had intense, dramatic handwriting. Seth Modine, I thought. It sounds like poetry.

Taking a deep breath, I scrawled my full name at the bottom of the sheet: Lily Rebecca Walker. I had practiced my signature a lot, and it looked pretty distinguished. Almost as stylish as Seth's.

"Just in time," Mrs. Cobb said, giving me a smile. "The first class is tomorrow. See you there."

"I signed up for a new writing class they're offering at South Regional," I said. I'd gone to the cemetery after school. I do that every now and then: visit my dad and sister's graves. And okay, call me crazy, but I talk to them.

Now I buttoned my coat up to the neck. It was a gray, bitterly cold afternoon. "I'm nervous about it, Daze. All the stories I've written up until now are so juvenile. What if people laugh at me?"

I was silent for a minute, listening as the wind rustled the last dry, papery-brown leaves on the branches of the beech tree next to the fence. A crow circled overhead, cawing mournfully. "You never had doubts like this, did you?" I asked finally. "I remember the way you used to look on the soccer field. Pure determination. I need to be more like that." I sighed. "Well, thanks for listening." I gave the two headstones a good-bye wave. "Love you, Daze. Love you, Daddy."

As I walked toward the gate snowflakes started to fall. "I'll let you know how it goes," I promised over my shoulder.

I was nervous about the writing workshop, but that didn't prevent me from dressing for the occasion: a narrow, knee-length skirt and a belted jacket, with my hair pinned up. Very 1930s and literary, I thought—Dorothy Parker. "I still can't believe you guys talked me into this," I hissed to Noelle and Mickey as we took seats in the next-to-last row of the classroom on Tuesday.

"You're going to love it," Mickey whispered back.

At that moment Seth and Timothy came in with a girl named Loryn Baker. I guess this is the right place to describe Seth Modine—not that mere words can do him justice. He's tall and lean, with one of those long, graceful bodies that clothes hang on really well. His hair is golden brown and longish, and he wears it swept back from his forehead in a very striking way. Behind his oval-rimmed glasses his eyes are dark gray, and he has a little cleft in his chin. He always wears trousers—never jeans. Today he was wearing a black mock turtleneck. He's way too cool for small-town Maine.

Timothy, Seth, and Loryn sat down right in front of us. "Hey," Timothy said to Noelle. She smiled at him. Seth met my eye briefly before dropping into his chair. My heart did a back flip.

"Yeah, maybe, I will" I was about to whisper

back to Mickey, but I kept the thought to myself. She'd leaned away from me to say something to Daniel Levin, who's also a tall, lean type but with reddish hair and blue eyes.

"Writers," Mrs. Cobb began, addressing us. "All of you are writers or want to become writers. The secret of writing is that anyone can do it. Talent is a mystery, but craft isn't. You learn by doing."

Mrs. Cobb talked for a while about what our assignments would be: recording conversations, brainstorming off different one-word topics, writing first-person essays and fiction. Sometimes we'd work in pairs so we could critique each other's stories.

"Today we're going to start with a loosening-up exercise," she went on. "We'll do these every class, and you'll do them on your own, too. The goal is to get you churning out a dozen pages a day. You won't love all of it—in fact, most of it will end up in the trash. But the more bad stuff you write, the more good stuff you'll write—the deeper you'll be digging into the well of material that everyone has inside. So, pick up your pens and turn to a blank piece of paper. Write a page about your bedroom. Describe things. Be concrete. I want to know what's in there, what it says about you."

I turned to Noelle. She wiggled her eyebrows. "What about *who's* in there?" she whispered.

I stifled a giggle.

"Let's not waste time chatting," Mrs. Cobb suggested, eyeing our part of the room.

Seth bent his head and started writing. I gripped my mechanical pencil, my own fingers itching. What had Mickey said? "You're going to love it. . . ."

I am, I realized. The assignments sounded fun, and it wouldn't kill me to spend fifty minutes twice a week staring at the back of Seth's head. And I could write a *book* about my bedroom.

I started scribbling. "*My room smells like faded roses and old books. It's jammed with stuff because I never throw anything away—broken dolls and tired stuffed animals perch on my windowsill, comfortable in the knowledge that I could never part with them.*"

I filled a page and flipped to the next. I couldn't believe I'd had doubts about taking this class. I can do this, I thought, exhilarated. I'm a writer. *That's* who I am!

After dinner I spent half an hour upstairs in my room on the phone with Noelle and Mickey, talking about the writing assignment. Then I sat at my desk with a new mechanical pencil and a narrow-ruled legal pad, waiting for inspiration. Mrs. Cobb wanted us to write about the ocean: either fiction or nonfiction, five pages. She figured that wouldn't be hard because we live right on the Atlantic—it's our world. Mickey had said she was going to write about clamming in Kettle Cove, and Noelle was going to write about this lifeguard she had a crush on one summer, but I didn't want to write about things that had actually happened to me. How boring.

Which isn't to say there aren't some dramatic episodes in my family history, I reflected. Dad's boat lost at sea, Daisy's car crash . . .

I shivered. I couldn't write about *that* stuff. It cut way too close to the bone. Maybe someone else's heartbreak, though . . .

I clicked my pencil twice so just the right amount of lead stuck out and started to write.

My short story, "Doomed," was ten pages long instead of five.

"Jeez," Noelle said, sneaking a peek before I handed it in to Mrs. Cobb. "What'd you do, write the Great American Novel?"

"It's pretty good," I had to admit.

"What's it about?" Mickey asked.

"It's a gothic romance set in nineteenth-century England," I told them. "This guy and this girl fall in love when he saves her from a shipwreck off the coast of Cornwall in which the rest of her family is drowned. But they keep getting separated by fate, and in the end, just as they're about to be reunited, she's run over by a train."

"Wow," Noelle said again. "You have an amazing imagination, Lily."

"Well, I borrowed the train part from *Anna Karenina*. I just hope Mrs. Cobb likes it," I said. "I think it's the most gripping story I've ever written."

The class spent the hour talking about "voice," and I spent the hour wondering what Seth Modine would look like with his black collarless shirt unbuttoned to the waist. I was also rehearsing what I'd say to Mrs. Cobb when she returned my assignment and said it was the best story in the class and she thought I should submit it to *The New Yorker.*

When Mrs. Cobb handed my story back next class, though, she didn't say anything about *The New Yorker.* She hadn't graded the assignment, and as I read her comments, I realized that was a lucky break. "*Unconvincing emotions . . . stilted dialogue . . . contrived situations,*" I read silently. "*Next time write in your own voice, Lily, and see what happens.*"

I frowned. Write in my own voice . . . what does *that* mean? Isn't pretending to be someone else what fiction is all about?

I planned to ask Mrs. Cobb about this at the end of class. At that moment she was looking for volunteers to read their assignments out loud. When no hands went up, she said, "Everyone will read eventually. Come on. Who's feeling brave today? I'd rather not have to call on you."

Mickey, Noelle, and I slumped down in our seats. Luckily Daniel saved us from a fate worse than death. "I'll read," he said.

"Excellent." Mrs. Cobb beamed at him. "Come on up and stand at the podium."

Daniel had written a nonfiction piece about going fishing with his grandfather. It was funny—the part about his grandfather bailing water out of the leaky old rowboat—and sad, too, because at the end it turned out his grandfather had just died and now Daniel had to go fishing by himself. "That was good," I whispered to Mickey. "Wasn't that good?"

Mickey nodded. "He had a lot of guts to go first."

I glanced at Daniel. He has that really fair complexion that auburn-haired people always have and he'd turned kind of magenta while he was reading, but now that he was back in his chair, he looked relieved. Our eyes met—his are dark blue—and I smiled. He smiled back.

I'll tell him I liked his story, I decided, but at that instant Daniel and his grandfather and the rowboat went right out of my brain. Mrs. Cobb had asked for another volunteer, and Seth had raised his hand.

Seth's story was about a spiritually tortured jazz musician living on the Left Bank in Paris. "I thought we were supposed to write about the ocean," Mickey hissed into my ear.

"Well, the Left Bank's on the Seine," I hissed back. "That's a body of water, anyway."

Seth's protagonist spent most of his time at cafes in soul-searching conversation with his equally tortured musician friends. I had no idea what Seth was getting at, but I loved the way he made intense eye contact with his audience, including me once or twice. Also, he had sprinkled real French throughout the dialogue. Basically I couldn't concentrate on much besides trying not to drool.

Seth finished reading. Mrs. Cobb said something polite, and he walked back to his seat.

At the end of class Mrs. Cobb randomly paired us up with writing partners. The idea was to get together with our partners between classes to share ideas, do writing exercises, and critique each other's stories. I held my breath as Mrs. Cobb read through her list. When she called out, "Lily Walker and Daniel Levin," I couldn't help letting out a sigh of disappointment. The very next pair was McKenna Clinton and Seth Modine. Mickey, who wouldn't even appreciate Seth at all!

"No way!" I hissed to Noelle.

"Life's so unfair!" she hissed back. Noelle hadn't even gotten a guy partner—she was paired with Beth Jacobs, a very serious, jockish girl.

The bell rang and I went up to Mrs. Cobb's desk. "I have a question," I said, waving "Doomed" at her. "You said to write in my own voice, but I'm not sure what you mean by that."

"Remember what we were talking about in class a few days ago?" she asked.

I didn't remember. I'd been too busy imagining what I would say to Seth if I ever got to speak to him. "Umm . . ."

"When you write in your own voice, you use language that comes naturally to you. You write about things you've experienced firsthand or situations you can fully imagine yourself in."

"You mean like Seth writing about jazz?" I asked.

At that moment Seth and Timothy walked by on their way to the door. Seth heard me talking about him and gave me a knowing half smile. I blushed furiously.

"Not exactly," Mrs. Cobb told me. "I don't mean that you should restrict yourself to everyday subjects. Fantasy is okay. Listen to yourself talk sometime, Lily. The rhythm, the diction. I liked the description of your bedroom. Try for some of that idiosyncratic flavor in your next story."

I thanked her for these pearls of wisdom even though I had no idea what she meant. Noelle and Mickey were waiting for me at the door. So was Daniel.

"Howdy, pardner," he cracked.

"Howdy, yourself," I said.

"Want to make a date?" He blushed when he realized what he'd said. "I mean, to get together and write?"

"Sure," I agreed. "I need all the help I can get!"

Daniel and I picked a time and place and he took off.

"Didn't Mrs. Cobb like the story you wrote?" Noelle asked me.

"She trashed it," I replied.

The three of us headed to our next class. "Wasn't Daniel's story good?" Mickey asked.

"How about Seth's?" Noelle countered.

"I thought Daniel's was better," Mickey said. "What did you think, Lily?"

I couldn't compare the stories because I didn't remember now if Seth's had been any good. "I liked Seth's use of *visual* imagery," I said meaning-fully.

My friends laughed.

At my locker I glanced again at Mrs. Cobb's comments on my shipwrecked-lovers story. Then I tossed the pages in with all the other junk on the locker floor.

Maybe being a great writer wasn't going to be as easy as I'd thought.

Four

That weekend Laurel came home from college for a visit. On Saturday she and Mom and I bundled up and went for a walk with Snickers along Lighthouse Road.

"I'm feeling down," Laurel announced when we got to the place where the road curves and there's a great view of the ocean.

Mom stopped to take off her gloves and hat. The sun was out, and it was turning into a mild winter afternoon. "What's wrong, honey?" she asked Laurel.

Laurel bent to pick up a stick. "I can't get over how bad my grades were last fall." She tossed the stick and Snickers bounded after it, barking. "My classes this semester are even harder. I'll probably flunk out."

"Your grades were *not* bad," Mom said firmly. "You're just not used to getting B's."

"And C's," Laurel said.

"It was *one* C-plus," Mom reminded her, "and in economics, which isn't even your major."

"But veterinary schools will look at *all* my grades," Laurel said glumly. "I'll never get in anywhere."

Mom hugged Laurel around the shoulders, laughing. "You're only a freshman—you have three more years to get that grade point up. College is harder than high school, that's all. You'll get the hang of it."

We kept walking. Maine is beautiful in the winter—in some ways I almost like it better than in the summer. With the trees bare you can see things more clearly, like the tumbling-down stone walls that zigzag through the woods, marking the boundaries of long-ago farms. Without green to compete with it, the sky and the water seem to have more color.

"Maybe you two can help me with something," Mom said. "The store needs a name. Any ideas?"

I thought about it. "Spice of Life," I suggested.

"Not bad," Mom said.

"The Sizzling Skillet," Laurel offered.

"The Plentiful Pantry," I said.

Mom laughed. "Don't get *too* carried away. I like the idea of a one-word name. Something simple but catchy."

Laurel lifted her shoulders. "I can't think of anything."

"It should be inviting, right?" I asked. "Something that makes people feel like they're sitting down to dinner with friends. How about . . . Potluck?"

"Potluck." Mom smiled. "I like that, Lily." She said it again. "Potluck. Yes, that could be it."

I got an unexpected thrill out of solving Mom's problem. "Anything else you need help with?" I asked.

"Actually, there is." She looked at Laurel rather than me, though. "I wanted to ask you about working for me this summer, Laurel. I know the Wildlife Rescue Center will have a job for you, but I'd like to make you assistant manager at the shop. I have a feeling that I'll really need the help."

"Really?" Laurel beamed. "I'd love to work at Potluck."

"What about me?" I broke in. "I'm sixteen. I could work for you, too, Mom. How about co-assistant manager?"

She was putting her hat back on; we were getting a sea breeze now and it was colder. "I'm sure there will be something for you to do, sweetheart," she said vaguely. I tried not to let my disappointment show.

At the driveway to the lighthouse we turned around. "How's school for *you* this term, Lil?" Laurel asked.

I told her about the writing class and Mrs. Cobb's not-so-hot response to my first story. "Your own voice, huh?" Laurel laughed. "That *would* be hard since you've always been the Girl of Many Disguises. I mean, how are you supposed to settle on just one?"

I sighed. "I have no idea. I have a writing partner now, though. This guy from the class—Daniel. I'm counting on him to help me. He's really good."

"Sorry for interrupting, Lil, but look." Mom pointed at something. "I didn't notice when we walked by in the other direction. The old place is for sale."

We peered through a brambly hedge at the three-story Victorian house where I'd lived as a child. It was a bed-and-breakfast now, the Lilac Inn, and a For Sale sign was planted on the lawn. "I can't believe it!" Laurel said.

"Why do you think they're going out of business?" I asked. "There are always tons of people staying there, at least in the summer."

Mom shook her head. "You never know. It might have nothing to do with how much money they're making. Things happen in people's lives that they have no control over." I knew she was thinking about Dad, remembering how tough it had been for us to make ends meet at first without him, and I reached for her hand.

"Who do you suppose will buy it next?" Laurel wondered, clipping Snickers's leash back on her collar. "Another innkeeper?"

"Maybe *we* could buy it!" I exclaimed.

"Wouldn't that be something?" Mom smiled wistfully. "Even if it's priced reasonably, though, we couldn't afford it right now. Hal and I are putting every penny into the new store."

We walked on toward town. I took a last look at the house over my shoulder, still holding Mom's hand. The wind was rocking the old porch swing—one of the few things the innkeepers had left unchanged when they fixed up the house. I remember sitting in that swing one summer day with Rose, I thought. We'd been stringing beads to make bracelets. Daisy was bouncing a ball against

the barn wall, Mom was gardening, Dad was
mending his fishing nets, and Laurel was climbing
an apple tree.

Our house, memories and all, was for sale again.

"Should we get something to eat, or are you
worried about smearing french fry grease on your
special narrow-ruled paper?"

"French fries sound great," I said. Daniel and I
were settled in a booth at Patsy's, the local diner,
our writing stuff spread out in front of us. "But
you'd better not make fun of my special paper, or
I'll make fun of your pencil case covered with smi-
ley face stickers that must date back to, like, second grade."

Daniel widened his eyes, playing dumb.
"Pencil case? What pencil case?"

I smiled and shook my head. Actually, now I
had to admit how lucky I was to have Daniel as a
writing partner—even though he wasn't Seth,
Daniel was nice. Plus I wasn't as distracted with
him as I would have been with Seth. We ordered a
basket of fries and some sodas. "Okay, so I'm totally clueless about this assignment," I told him. It
was Sunday night—we had five pages to write for
Tuesday. "Mrs. Cobb is so obtuse. Write about disappointment. What does *that* mean?"

Daniel laughed. He has a nice laugh. "You've
never been disappointed?" he asked, raising one
sandy-red eyebrow in this very comical look.

I laughed, too. "Yeah, sure. But I mean, do we

write about one disappointment or about disappointment in general?"

"I guess you write about whatever it means to you," Daniel replied. "I think that's why Mrs. Cobb gives these open-ended assignments. She leaves room to experiment."

I sighed. "I'd feel better if she spelled it out. I bombed out last time—I don't want to turn in another crummy piece."

"Well, I'm not sure what to write about, either. Maybe we should start with one of those brainstorming exercises." He shoved a couple of fries in his mouth, then reached for his notebook and a pen. "Let's brainstorm on the word *disappointment* for five minutes and see what we come up with."

I grabbed my pencil. "Ready, set, go."

We both paused for a second, thinking, and then started writing as fast as we could. The brainstorming thing really does work. When you brainstorm, you don't really pay attention to the words you're putting on the page—they just pour out. Then you read it afterward and it's kind of a surprise.

"Five minutes are up," Daniel announced after what felt like five seconds. "Do you want to read yours out loud first or shall I?"

"Read it out *loud?*" I repeated.

"Sure. That's what we're supposed to be doing. That's how we can help each other."

I shook my head. "I think I'll just look this over at home later and see if it gives me any ideas."

"Uh-uh," Daniel said firmly. "We're writing

partners, Lily. Believe me, I feel dumb about reading mine out loud, too. In class the other day I almost passed out, I was so nervous. But it's really helpful." His voice softened. "You can trust me. I won't say anything harsh."

I looked into Daniel's eyes. He looked totally sincere and kind. "Well . . . okay," I said. "Let me eat some french fries first, though. I want to die on a full stomach."

We finished off the fries. Then Daniel read his page of brainstorming. Then I read mine. And you know what? It wasn't the worst thing in the world. I blushed a little and I couldn't stop fidgeting with a strand of my hair, but I read the whole thing.

"That's the first time in my *life* that anyone's heard something I've written," I told Daniel, "except for the time my big sister Rose found my story notebook when I was about eight and read the whole thing."

"Well, how'd the excercise feel?" Daniel asked.

"A little embarrassing," I confessed. "But not as embarrassing as I expected. I mean, I didn't even realize I'd written that stuff about being the last one in my junior high clique to get my ears pierced."

Daniel and I high-fived each other. "Now we just need to figure out what would be a good story idea. You're going to write about that junior high stuff, right?" he kidded.

I groaned. "A work of genius in the rough," I joked. But honestly, being with Daniel, I somehow felt it might be.

*　　*　　*

Daniel and I spent about fifteen more minutes at the diner. Back at home later I turned on my computer to write in my journal. *"What's shaking?"* I typed. *"Mrs. Cobb hated my first story. Was it really that bad? I thought the train crash scene was particularly vivid and gory, and the period costume details were excellent. Actually, Mrs. Cobb did like the costume stuff—she's into specifics, like the way things smell and feel and taste. But it all comes back to the voice thing. I forgot to ask Daniel's opinion about that. What kind of voice am I supposed to use? Should I scream? Whisper? Whine? Yodel?"*

I spent a few minutes describing my walk with Mom and Laurel and my writing date with Daniel. *"Daniel's a really good writer,"* I typed, *"and he's also a good listener. He doesn't make snap judgments. Which isn't to say that he only said nice things about stuff I wrote tonight, but he was constructive. I think I lucked out getting him as a writing partner. I still haven't decided what to write about for class, though."*

I switched off the computer and sat at my desk with pencil and paper. I'm not sure why, but that's how I do it: I type my journal and handwrite everything else. Now I closed my eyes, trying to visualize a story and a voice telling that story. It needs to be completely different, I thought. Not gothic and romantic like "Doomed." Something totally nontraditional.

I experimented with a sentence or two. "The girl stood at the bus stop in the rain. Her shoulders were hunched, and wet strands of dirty blond hair fell over eyes that were blank with despair. She waited."

I frowned down at the page. "It needs more drama," I said to myself. "What if I . . ."

Tearing off a new sheet of paper, I rewrote it without using capitals or punctuation. "the girl stood at the bus stop in the rain her shoulders were hunched and wet strands of dirty blond hair fell over eyes that were blank with despair she waited."

I smiled. I like that, I decided. Talk about different!

My new writing style seemed to require a new look, so on Tuesday, I wore a short, shapeless black dress and tights with holes in them and pale makeup with very dark lipstick. I pulled my hair back in a tight ponytail and wore earrings that were so long, they almost hit my shoulders. The finishing touch was a pair of glasses with black rectangular frames and clear lenses that I'd picked up at Second Time Around.

"Wow. Look at you," Noelle said as we met at my locker before writing class. "Why so ghoulish?"

I hesitated for an instant, then thrust my pages at Noelle and Mickey. No point in being shy. I'd already read it over the phone to Daniel, and Mrs. Cobb would see it soon—it was time for my story to fend for itself. "Here. Read this."

Mickey and Noelle stood side by side to read together. "Do you like it?" I asked hopefully when they got to the last page.

Mickey nodded. "It's grim and bleak and

depressing. You can really feel the emotions, you know? And the way she doesn't have a name. She's just 'the girl.'"

"It's cool," Noelle agreed. "Like something you'd read in a magazine. Sophisticated."

I beamed. I thought so, too. "I'm glad you guys like it. Daniel wasn't so positive."

"What does he know?" Noelle asked.

"Anyway, it's the exact opposite of my other story stylistically," I explained, "so Mrs. Cobb is bound to like it."

"You should read it aloud in class," Mickey said.

I shook my head.

"Come on," Noelle urged.

"I'm not ready," I said as we headed into the room.

"*I'd* volunteer if my story were that good," Mickey said.

We sat at the opposite end of the third row from Seth and Timothy because Timothy had asked Noelle out again and she'd said no. Apparently even though he was *almost* as good-looking as Seth, Timothy's lips were simply too gooey. Noelle had also decided he was atrociously stuck on himself.

As Mrs. Cobb chatted about today's focus, the character arc, I thought about my friends urging me to read. I kept turning my head to gaze at Seth's gorgeous profile. At one point he looked my way and our eyes met, and he actually gave me a little smile.

I slumped in my chair, clutching my story with sweaty hands. I'd love to impress Seth—especially with my writing. But what if I fell flat on my face? He was so intellectual. My story had *no* references to philosophy or French or foreign films or anything like that, like Seth's had the other day. If he thinks it stinks, I'll die, I thought.

Mrs. Cobb finished writing on the blackboard and turned to face the class. "Who'd like to read first today?"

I was sitting in between Noelle and Mickey—I got an elbow from each side. "Ouch!" I whispered.

"Go for it," Noelle whispered into one ear.

"Everyone has to sometime," Mickey hissed into the other ear.

I cast an anguished glance at Seth, who was drumming his fingers on his desk in a bored fashion. Mickey was right. I had to read sometime. Why not get it over with?

"I—I'll read, Mrs. C-Cobb," I stammered, raising my hand.

"Lily. Wonderful."

I walked up to the podium, painfully conscious that all eyes in the room were on me. My legs buckled slightly. So that's what it means to have your knees knock, I thought, doing my best not to trip.

I stepped behind the podium and then turned around to face the class. "Uh-hmm," I said, clearing my throat. "My story, on the theme of disappointment, is titled 'Runaway to Nowhere.'" I pushed my fake glasses up on the bridge of my nose. "Before I start, I want to say that there's something you won't get by just listening to this, but it's all in lowercase with no punctuation." I caught Daniel's eye, and even though I knew he thought my story was crummy (well, he'd put it much nicer, but that had been the general idea), he gave me an encouraging smile. "So maybe just think about how that might affect the story's mood, you know? Okay." I cleared my throat yet again. "Here goes."

I started reading, keeping my voice flat and somber to match the all-lowercase/no-punctuation thing. I read really slowly to give all the words the proper emphasis. "the girl stood at the bus stop in the rain her shoulders were hunched and wet strands of dirty blond hair fell over eyes that were blank with despair she waited."

I paused, daring to look up at the class. Seth's expression was unreadable; Loryn was studying a chip in her dark blue fingernail polish. At least Daniel, Noelle, and Mickey appeared interested. "when the bus pulled up the girl got on without even looking at the destination she didn't care where it was headed as long as it took her away from her life her painful lonely desperate life."

I kept reading, my manner exaggeratedly serious to go with the material. Then I heard a sound—the worst possible sound you can hear when you're reading one of your stories out loud in class for the first time in your life.

Someone snickered.

Mrs. Cobb murmured, "Sshh."

Swallowing, I went on reading.

Someone else snickered.

"Please listen quietly," Mrs. Cobb requested.

My face turned red with mortification, but I was stuck up there, less than halfway through my story. "she thought it would be different in a new place with new people but she'd brought her problems her fears her disappointment with her," I read. "the loneliness was larger than an ocean and sucked her down like a vortex she struggled against the current but she was helpless helplessly struggling helpless."

Someone laughed out loud. It was Loryn. She clapped a hand over her mouth, but she couldn't stop giggling. I kept reading, but the more serious and sad the stuff in my story was, the more people laughed.

Mrs. Cobb, Mickey, Noelle, and Daniel seemed to be the only ones in the whole room with straight faces. Mickey darted angry glances at the laughers; Noelle bit her lip. I could tell she was feeling awful for me. My eyes prickled and my throat grew tight. It's not supposed to be funny! I wanted to cry out.

I wanted to burst into tears and run out of the room, but I knew that would make me look even more like an idiot. I stood there, frozen, for what felt like a year but was probably only two or three seconds. What am I doing wrong? I wondered. I kept reading mechanically as my mind spun. Why is this different from when Daniel and Seth and other people stood up to read? Why don't I ever hit the right note?

Then suddenly I thought about a story Loryn had read last class. It had been kind of mean—she'd been making fun of a fat girl who went to the same diner every day and ordered the same enormous meal and ate all the food in the same order and folded her napkin in the same exact way every time. People had laughed, but not *at* her, the way they were now, with my story. Maybe I'm taking myself too seriously, I thought. Being sincere is uncool.

All at once I had a brilliant idea. I kept reading my story and the class kept laughing, so I started playing it that way, as if I'd *meant* to be hilarious. "she stood on the banks of the river and thought about throwing herself in how the cold water would close over her head and she could finally forget the other deeper coldness of the people who didn't care." I made my tone ironic and raised one eyebrow slightly. "but she lacked the courage to take that ultimate step she lacked the courage even to get back on the bus and return to the place where all her unhappiness had begun."

I threw in some body language and changed my voice to sound a bit more like Cruella De Vil. I heard the laughter change; they were laughing *with* me, as they had with Loryn. Seth leaned forward to listen, his elbows on his desk, his lips curved in an appreciative smile. My story had turned into a comedy routine. I was a hit.

When I read the last sentence—"she'd learned nothing gone nowhere become no one"—the class actually clapped. I gave a bow and went back to my seat. "Awesome, Lil!" Noelle whispered, squeezing my arm. "We were worried about you for a minute there, but you really pulled it off."

I darted a glance down the row at Seth. He smiled at me, an interested light in his gray eyes. That was a Look, I thought, my heart cartwheeling around in my chest. Seth Modine just gave me a Look!

After class a bunch of kids surrounded me at the door. "That was *so* funny," Loryn declared. "My sides are still aching."

"You should try out for the talent show," suggested Rico Chivetti, this cute theater guy who's part of the It crowd. "I'm one of the judges. You'd be a shoo-in."

"I'll think about it," I said casually.

Usually I walk to my next class with Mickey, but today I was part of a big, lively, laughing group. Seth and Timothy kind of brought up the rear, but you would definitely have had to say that we were walking together. I'm part of a group with Seth, I thought dizzily.

"See you, Lily," Loryn said when we got to her locker.

Seth's locker was a couple down from Loryn's. "Later, Lily," he said.

"Bye," I replied, breathless with happiness and disbelief.

"Don't forget the talent show," Rico called.

I gave him a wave. The talent show, I thought. He wants me to try out for the talent show! And Seth spoke to me! He said my name!

I'd been teetering on the edge of disaster, but miraculously I'd turned things around. Noelle and Mickey had been right when they'd talked me into taking the writing class.

I'd finally found a way to stand out. And I planned to keep it that way.

Five

It wasn't hard to immerse myself in my new identity. I went to Second Time Around with an armful of Victorian-style dresses and came home with all black clothes. I wore the rectangular glasses all the time and dark eyeliner and lipstick that Noelle and Mickey told me was "scary, but in a good way." And I wrote all my stories for Mrs. Cobb's class in lowercase letters with no punctuation, and they were all about alienated kids, and they all sounded depressing on paper but were hilarious when read aloud in a certain sarcastic tone that I was rapidly perfecting, and I volunteered to read aloud all the time now even though I didn't have to. Because the class *loved* my stories.

One Wednesday, when I didn't have writing class during lunch, I walked alone to the cafeteria. Right outside the door I bumped into Daniel. "Hey," he said.

"Hey," I said back.

"Getting something to eat?"

"The thought had occurred to me," I replied.

He held the door open for me. "That's a lot of black you've got on."

I shrugged. "They're clothes. They cover my essential nakedness."

Daniel laughed. We stepped into the food line, and he gave my shoulder a playful little bump. "You don't have to put on an act with *me*, Lily."

I bumped his shoulder back. "What act?"

"For one thing, the glasses." He pointed to them. "I thought they were just a prop, for your story. But you're still wearing them."

I lifted a hand to touch the glasses self-consciously. "Eyewear is an accessory just like, you know, a belt or earrings."

"Oh. I see," Daniel said.

He was still smiling. I tried to give him a withering glance, but I couldn't. Instead I felt like giggling. The glasses *were* a little over the top. "Who are you eating with?" I asked. "Do you want to have lunch?"

"Actually, I'm grabbing a sandwich to take with me to the computer lab—I have a project to finish," Daniel said. "Rain check, okay?"

"Rain check," I agreed warmly.

Daniel paid for his lunch and took off. There was a very brief interlude where I was standing alone with my tray, feeling dopey about the fact that I had to look for someone to join, and then Loryn swept me off to her table. *Seth's* table.

Not only was I sitting at the see-and-be-seen crowd's usual highly visible table by the window, but I was sitting next to Seth. I wasn't exactly sure how that happened, if it was an accident or on purpose.

Anyway, there I was, trying to look casual while inside I felt like a six-year-old who'd managed to get her paws in an impossible-to-reach cookie jar.

"You're going to *die* over this," Loryn said to the group in her typically bored tone. "I've been asked to join the *prom* committee."

"The prom committee," Rico said. "What an honor."

Loryn rolled her dark-lined eyes expressively. "Isn't it? Staci Shipman asked me herself." She launched into an imitation of Staci, the unbelievably perky president of the pep club. "'You'd be *really* good at picking the chaperons, Loryn, because you're *really* smart and all the teachers *really* like you! Just remember it's *really* important to have *really* cool chaperons so we can all *really* have fun at the dance that will, like, *really* be our very best memory of high school!'"

"Does Staci always sound like she just sucked the helium out of a balloon or what?" Timothy wanted to know. "I hope you have a great time working with her on the prom committee."

"I can't wait to join—it's going to be hilarious. I've always wanted an inside look at the pep club. I mean, how do these people *think?*"

"Do they think, period?" Rico wondered.

"Anyway, I have some great ideas for chaperons." Her eyes twinkled darkly. "Mr. Adams."

Everybody hooted. Mr. Adams is the very large, very hairy metal shop teacher. He rides a Harley.

"And Mrs. Balicki," Loryn went on. More laughter—Mrs. Balicki is about eighty.

"Mr. Simonides," I suggested. This went over well, too. Mr. Simonides is the social studies teacher who must smoke three packs of unfiltered Camel cigarettes a day.

"Ms. Carpenter," Timothy put in. "I bet she can really dance."

There were more chuckles, but my own smile faltered. This didn't strike me as funny at all. Ms. Carpenter uses a wheelchair.

Before I could speak up, Seth told Loryn, "Make sure you ask Mrs. Cobb."

"Right, and I'll tell her that in between the band's sets, we all want to pair up for brainstorming exercises. Speaking of Mrs. Cobb, who here has a lame writing partner?" Loryn asked, raising her own hand.

Seth raised his. "You don't like working with Mickey?" I asked, surprised. Mickey's about the nicest, most thoughtful person on the planet.

"I'm sorry, I know she's your bud, but she can't write," Seth said. He leaned back in his chair, his linked hands clasped behind his neck. "And if you can't write, you can't give a legitimate critique. Not that that stops her. But *you're* stuck with Levin." Seth made a tsk, tsk sound with his tongue.

I thought about how I could defend my friends in a tactful way that didn't make me sound like a puritan. But I was too busy feeling relieved. Thank goodness Seth didn't see me in the lunch line with Daniel before, I thought.

We spent the rest of lunch period ripping apart Hawk Harbor. I've always liked my hometown, but Seth and his buddies had a much hipper attitude. Hawk Harbor was provincial, boring, tacky, and anti-intellectual. That's why they hung out at a coffee bar in Kent instead of at one of the usual teen spots like Pizza Bowl or the Rusty Nail. "Our goal is to live in Maine without actually *living* in Maine," Seth explained to me. "No lobster fishing for us."

"You're expatriates," I said.

He laughed. "Exactly."

We looked at each other. I was kind of spellbound by how brilliant his eyes looked behind those glasses.

Apparently he was looking at my glasses, too. "Nice specs," he said.

"Oh, these." I prayed he couldn't tell that the lenses were fake. "Thanks."

"So, come with us sometime," Loryn invited me. "To the coffee shop."

I breathed deeply to keep myself from clapping with glee. "Sure," I said.

"I can't believe you sat with those guys at lunch," Mickey said later as we rode the school bus.

I shrugged. "It's no big deal."

"Just don't forget about your old friends, okay?"

"Of course not." I punched her lightly on the arm. "Don't be silly." I felt momentarily disloyal, remembering how I'd let Seth and Loryn's cracks about Mickey and Daniel slide. "Next time I'm with them, you could sit with us," I offered, even though I kind of hoped she wouldn't. "You don't *have* to hang out with Daniel and the geeks."

Mickey gave me a stern look. "Daniel's not a geek," she said. "He's my friend. Okay?"

"I'm just kidding," I assured her. "I like him. But you should really spend some time with me and Loryn and Rico and Seth." I blushed a little, just saying his name. "They're really fun to be around."

"I'm sure they are," Mickey said. I couldn't read her expression.

The bus stopped on Main Street a block away from my apartment. Mickey was coming over to work on a math problem set with me.

We settled down in the family room with our math textbooks and notebooks spread open. Every time we started to make some progress on the homework assignment, though, the phone would ring. First it was Loryn, "just calling to talk before tackling the intellectual challenge of homework." Then Rico called to remind me about the talent show tryouts the next day. Finally Fiona Sullivan called.

"Hi," I said, surprised. I couldn't imagine why Fiona would be calling *me*. She's possibly the coolest junior girl at South Regional. We're in the same homeroom, but we hardly ever talk to each other. The only connection between us is that about a million years ago, her older brother Brian dated my big sister Rose. "What's up?" I asked.

"I wanted to tell you I'm having a party Friday night," Fiona said. "You're not busy, are you?"

"No. I mean, I don't think so," I added, so I wouldn't sound *too* available.

"Good. Seth will be there. Bring some friends along if you like. It'll be fun."

"Great. Thanks."

"See you in homeroom."

"Right. Bye, Fiona."

Mickey's dark eyebrows arched up so high, they almost disappeared into her hair. "Fiona?"

I nodded.

"Fiona *Sullivan?*"

"Yep."

Mickey shook her head. "Wow. You *have* arrived."

"She's having a party on Friday, and she said I should bring some friends. Do you want to come with me?"

Mickey shrugged. "I wouldn't know what to do with myself at a party at Fiona's. I mean, I'm not that good at talking to Beautiful People."

"That's ridiculous," I said. "They're not Beautiful, and you talk to them just like you talk to anybody." Even as I said this, though, I knew it wasn't true. Fiona and Seth and their circle *were* Beautiful—capital *B*. And I never *used* to know how to talk to them, I thought. Not until lately. Not until reading my story in creative-writing class changed everything.

Mickey and I got back to work. When we were done with math, we sat on the couch with our writing notebooks and read each other our stories in progress. "Your stuff is getting wilder and wilder," Mickey commented when I finished reading my latest masterpiece, which was about this girl who goes from guy to guy seeking love and self-affirmation, but it doesn't work, and along the way she gets anorexic. In the end she starts eating again and gives up boys, and there's just the faintest hint that she might figure herself out. "At least that one has sort of a happy ending."

"Don't you think it's funny?" I asked. "You're supposed to be laughing your head off."

"I smiled a little," Mickey said. "What did you think of *my* story?"

I gave Mickey my most constructive criticism in case she read her story to Seth at some point. She's pretty imaginative, but for some reason that doesn't always come out in her writing. After she left and before dinner, with my stomach growling in appropriate fashion, I put a few finishing touches on "Hunger" and then called up Daniel to invite him over later for microwave popcorn and a critique session. He suggested going out someplace in town, like the diner again, but I didn't really want anyone to see us together even though we *were* just writing partners.

When he showed up at seven-thirty, I introduced him to my mother and Hal and then we shut ourselves up in the family room. As we got

comfortable on the couch, kicking off our shoes
and slumping side by side into the pillows with our
feet on the coffee table, Daniel joked, "Aren't they
going to wonder what we're up to in here?"

"Please." I rolled my eyes, Loryn style. "Are
you ready to hear my latest?"

He nodded. "Hit me."

I read the story in my most dryly sarcastic
tone, the one that always made people laugh.
Daniel didn't even crack a grin. "You're grumpier
than Mickey," I complained. "How about a chuckle
or two?"

He let out a long sigh. "I guess I don't get it,"
he confessed. "I know everybody else thinks the
stuff you're writing these days is a riot, but it
leaves me . . . I don't know." He shrugged. "It
feels hollow or something. Like you're not writing
about people you care about. It's just to get a
laugh."

I blew out a frustrated puff of air. "But I'm trying so *hard*." I wasn't sure why, but I wanted
Daniel to like my story. "Are you sure you don't
think it's a *little* funny?"

"Why does it have to be funny?" he countered.

"I don't know." I thought about it. "Because I
like making people laugh?"

I phrased it as a question, but Daniel didn't answer me. "What does Mrs. Cobb think?" he said
instead.

I blew out another puff of air. "She's still coming down hard on me. You know what she's like.

She always makes a point of saying a couple of nice things. But most of her comments are negative. You know what, though?" I slapped my notebook down on the couch. "I don't care. Everyone else will like it, right?"

"What about you, though? Do *you* like it?"

"I wrote it," I reminded him.

"Yeah, but that doesn't mean it *moves* you."

I lifted my notebook again, covering my face with it. "Can we not be so New Age touchy-feely?" I begged.

When I peeked around the edge of the notebook, Daniel was grinning at me, one strand of auburn hair flopping into his eyes. "I just want you to be in harmony with your inner music."

I groaned. "Okay, if you're so harmonized, read me what *you* wrote."

Our assignment was to write about food, which is how I'd come up with my anorexia theme. Daniel had written about a Thanksgiving dinner at his cousins' when he was ten. It was a sweet, touching story, and when he was done, I actually sniffled.

"You're good at doing that twist thing at the end," I said. Daniel offered me a tissue from the box on the end table. "You know, how we think it's going to be sad because the dog just died and then your uncle who nobody's seen in years shows up and surprises everybody."

"Yeah, well, thanks." Daniel's cheeks turned pink; he sounded pleased.

"Not that it's perfect." I didn't want him to get lazy. "You need to use more action verbs, and you've *got* to get rid of that passive voice stuff, like, 'the ball was thrown by so and so' and 'the feeling was experienced by such and such.'"

"Right." Daniel scribbled something in his notebook. "Thanks."

Twenty minutes later I walked Daniel to the door. "Night," I said.

"Night," he echoed. "Uh, Lily?"

"Yeah?"

"Would you ever want to . . . uh . . . instead of just getting together to write . . . maybe try to . . . um . . ."

I waited patiently, but he didn't go on. "Was that a question?" I prodded.

"Sort of." He blushed furiously. "But I think I'll ask it some other time. See you tomorrow."

"So long," I told him, thinking how weird guys could be.

As soon as the door closed behind him I got it. Daniel was about to ask me out! I decided it was just as well he hadn't gone through with it because of course I couldn't say yes. I hope things don't end up getting awkward between us, I thought.

I didn't dwell on it for long. I was concentrating on rereading my story. Daniel and Mickey didn't like it, and Mrs. Cobb probably won't, either, I mused, but I bet the rest of the class will think it's great. "And Seth's the one who speaks French and wants to go to film school," I said to myself as I stapled the pages together. Mrs. Cobb and Daniel were entitled to their opinions, but I wasn't going to cry over them. What did *they* know?

"I thought I'd find you here," a voice behind me said.

I whirled around. Lately instead of pulling my hair back in a severe ponytail, I'd been wearing it down, kind of hanging over my face. Now it whirled with me like a windblown curtain, and my rectangular spectacles slipped halfway down the bridge of my nose. "Seth," I squeaked. "Hi!"

I was standing in the back of the high school auditorium, watching kids audition for the talent show. I'd already had my tryout, and I thought it had gone pretty well. Rico and the rest of the judges had laughed really hard at my poem, "Up and Down and Down Some More."

Seth dropped into a seat near me, slumping down comfortably. He was wearing charcoal gray trousers with a muted dark teal and black plaid oxford buttoned all the way up. He had his glasses off and was twirling them kind of the way a lifeguard twirls a whistle. As those intense eyes drank me up, I felt like I was onstage again. Onstage without any clothes on.

"How'd it go?" he asked.

"Okay," I said, thinking, Thank goodness he didn't show up *before* my audition. I'd have been dumbstruck. "We'll see, right?"

"Right." Seth glanced at the stage. A girl was

twirling the baton. "She should do the world a favor and toss that thing in the harbor," he said.

I had to laugh. "Cut her some slack. It takes guts just to get up there."

He nodded, his eyes on me again. "True, I suppose. Were *you* nervous?"

Not as nervous as I am now, I thought. "No," I said nonchalantly. "If I get a spot, great. If not, I'll live. Why are you here, anyway? Are you auditioning?"

Seth laughed. "And what would I do?"

As far as I was concerned, Seth could just get up onstage and let people look at him. But when I thought about it, I couldn't actually picture him performing. "I'm stumped," I admitted.

"My point exactly," Seth said.

"But if you really wanted to, I'm sure you could juggle or whistle or sing 'My Heart Will Go On,' couldn't you?" I teased.

"I love all the junk people consider talent. It's so unbelievably clichéd. Except for you. You're a cut above the rest."

"Yeah?" I couldn't believe Seth was saying such nice things about me—and I was dying to hear more.

He didn't disappoint me. "You project so much wit and acuity."

I made a mental note to look up *acuity* in a dictionary later. "Well . . . ," I murmured, my eyelashes lowered modestly.

"So, Lily, the real reason I'm here . . ." Seth dropped his voice. It was as warm and deep as velvet.

I wanted to *wear* it. "Would you like to go to Fiona's party with me tomorrow night?"

"W-what?" I stammered, convinced my hearing had failed me. Or maybe I was just losing my mind.

"Fiona's party tomorrow night. She told me she invited you. Do you want to go together?"

The lights in the auditorium were dim, but I could tell my face was glowing like a neon sign. "Uh . . . yes," I finally managed to say. "Sure. It sounds like fun." I bit my lip before I could say any more dorky-sounding things.

"I'll pick you up at eight. Where do you live?"

"In town, right over Wissinger's Bakery. The name's on the bell."

Getting to his feet, Seth touched my arm lightly. "See you in school tomorrow."

"Yeah," I managed to choke out.

I watched him walk out of the auditorium. I still hadn't decided what was more amazing about him: his body or his wardrobe. The combination was devastating, that was for sure.

Oh, wow, I thought, sinking weakly into a seat. If I'd been a heroine in a nineteenth-century novel, I would have fainted dead away. I have a date tomorrow night with Seth Modine!

"I have a date with Seth Modine tomorrow night!" I screamed over the phone to Noelle half an hour later.

"I can't believe it!" she screamed back.

We screamed for another minute. My body was

so full of adrenaline, I could have sprinted to Portland and back without breaking a sweat. I still couldn't get over what had just happened.

"So, wait," Noelle commanded. "Tell me again, word for word. I want to know every single thing he said, what he looked like, what you said and what you looked like, et cetera."

I repeated the story, going into as much delicious detail as possible. "I can't believe it!" Noelle screamed again at the end.

"Me either!" I screamed.

I was still hyped about it the next day. When Seth sat next to me in creative writing, I nearly fell off my chair. Every time I glanced through my clear lenses at Mickey and Noelle, who were sitting on the other side of me, they wiggled their eyebrows and I'd almost burst out laughing. Having Seth so close made my temperature rise about ten degrees. I literally felt feverish.

Then at the end of the day, the principal announced the names of the kids who'd gotten spots in the talent show. I stood by my locker with Noelle and Mickey, listening. The three of us held hands, and when we heard my name, we lifted our joined hands in the air and screamed. There'd been a lot of screaming going on lately.

"You did it, Lil!" Mickey shrieked.

Noelle flung her arms around me. "Congratulations!"

We spun in a circle, all hugging. "I can't believe it," I said.

"Things are totally clicking for you these days," Noelle observed.

I nodded. It was almost too much to take in. The talent show and Seth. "I can't believe just a few weeks ago I was feeling like a nobody."

"And look at you now," Mickey said. "Queen of South Regional!"

"Mickey was only half joking," I wrote in my journal later on at home. *"I don't want my old friends to think my ego's getting out of control, though, so I assured her it was just 'Queen for a Day.' But you know what, Diary? I'll take my fifteen minutes of fame. It's so great to be in the center of things instead of on the outside. To know for the first time in my life that other people are looking at me with envy. Maybe that's totally shallow. So, shoot me. It's the way I feel."*

I exited my journal and shut down my computer. "Now I know what it was like to be you," I said softly, my eyes on Daisy's picture. "To be a winner."

I spent about two hours getting ready for my date with Seth. It wasn't like I'd never had a date before—I'd gone out with plenty of guys, a couple of whom had even qualified as boyfriends. But I'd never gone out with anyone as sophisticated as Seth. He was in a completely different league, and I didn't want to blow it. I wanted him to ask me out again. And again and again and again . . .

I wish I had a big sister around, I thought in the shower. Even Laurel would have been better than nothing, even though her fashion sense is nonexistent. But it was really Daisy I longed to share this with. I wanted her to see how well I was turning out.

I washed my hair and shaved my legs and scrubbed myself all over with this foamy peach-scented body wash I borrowed from Mom. Afterward I blew-dry my hair so it would be really straight and put on body lotion and deodorant. Finally, wearing a bra and underwear, I went into my closet.

This was the hard part. I had so many great clothes. What should I wear?

I fingered a green velour swing dress. That was cute. Or what about hip-hugger jeans with a really cool top? My suede-fringed skirt looks good on me, I thought, and so does that white sailor-collar blouse. But I also liked the electric blue jumper and the green wrap miniskirt and the . . .

Then I remembered. Seth had started paying attention to me when I started dressing in black and wearing spectacles and acting cynical. Nobody in the It crowd sported cowboy boots. If I wear pink, I realized, Seth won't recognize me.

So I put on a short black skirt, a skinny black T-shirt, black tights, and black shoes. Even my earrings were black. The only thing that wasn't black was my hair, which I wore parted in the middle and combed straight down so that it hid half my face. I didn't put on perfume—it seemed too adolescent.

"I thought you had a date," Mom said as I sat

down next to her on the living room couch to wait for Seth.

"I do."

Mom frowned a little. "That's what you're wearing?"

"What's wrong with it?"

"You have so many *pretty* clothes."

"Mom, I'm nervous," I said. "Please don't give me a hard time."

"Sorry, hon." She gave me a hug, carefully, so that she wouldn't mess up my hair. "I just didn't recognize you. You're usually so colorful."

"Black is always in style," I reminded her.

When the doorbell rang, I shot to my feet as if I'd been launched by a space shuttle rocket. "It's *him*," I announced, my voice cracking inelegantly.

Mom followed me into the hallway. "Do *I* get to meet him?" she asked.

"Of course," I said, but my hand was shaking too much to turn the knob. "Help me, Mom," I whispered.

Mom opened the door. "You must be Seth," she said, giving him a warm smile.

They shook hands. "It's a pleasure to meet you, Mrs. Walker," Seth said. "This is a great apartment. It must be intense living over the bakery— all those evocative smells. Like Proust and his madeleines, right?"

"Proust?" Mom asked.

He's so smart, I thought, hoping Mom was soaking it in. I tried not to look too smug. I really couldn't get over this. A cultured, gorgeous, ultracool guy was here to take *me* on a date. Unbelievable!

Seth explained his Proust reference, tossing out lots of long words along the way. Mom nodded. "I see what you mean," she said with another smile.

I stepped forward, clutching my coat and purse. "Ready to go?" I asked.

I got over my nervousness pretty quickly during the car ride to Fiona's. Seth and I started talking, and it was just like reading my stories in Mrs. Cobb's class. I put on a careless, cynical tone and joked about everything. I made Seth laugh.

I kept it up at Fiona's party. It was a little harder because Seth put his arm around me and that momentarily short-circuited my brain, but pretty soon I was back in the groove. It was like there was a CD inside me and someone had pushed the play button. No matter what people were talking about—music, movies, school—I had something sarcastic and unexpected to say on the subject. Together Seth and I were definitely the It couple of the evening.

Not that this was necessarily quite the thrill I'd expected it to be. I'd never partied with these people before, and I'd thought they'd be a little more . . . lively. A little more fun. No one danced, though, and when I suggested ducking outside for a moonlit walk—Fiona lives a block from the ocean—Seth just yawned. "I'm happy here," he said, indicating his place on the couch. "Moonlight's overrated, if you ask me."

So we sat on the couch with a bunch of his friends and talked. And talked. When I was sure we'd covered every topic in the universe, we found some new ones and talked some more. It was exhilarating to talk to people who had so much to say, but it was exhausting, too. Because I knew I had to stay on my toes. Say the right thing, everybody loves you, I figured out. Say the wrong thing, and next time *you'll* be the one they rake over the coals.

Seth drove me home at quarter to twelve because I had a midnight curfew. "We still have a few minutes," he said, parking by the curb in front of the bakery and turning off the engine.

I unbuckled my belt and turned a little in my seat to face him. "Thanks for the fun evening," I said softly.

"Thank *you*." Seth put out a hand and gently brushed my hair back from my face. "You know, you're as beautiful as you are sharp. That's a rare combination."

"Oh, well," I said nonchalantly.

Seth's hand moved to my shoulders. He pulled me gently toward him. "May I kiss you?"

I nodded yes. We tried a brief, experimental kiss . . . and liked it. So we tried another one. Seth wasn't the first boy I'd kissed, but he was far and away the sexiest. Kissing him wasn't like anything I'd ever experienced. Our mouths fit together perfectly, and so did our bodies, and when he wrapped me up in his arms with his lips on mine, I felt pretty sure I'd died and gone to heaven.

"Look," Seth said. He'd left the key half turned in the ignition so we could read the clock on the dashboard. It read 12:00.

"Time flies," I said with a sigh.

He mussed my hair. "There. Now you look like you've really been up to something you shouldn't."

I laughed. "Thanks."

We kissed again, just a light brush of the lips that still felt remarkably electric. "See you," I said casually.

"Maybe later this weekend," he agreed. "I'll call you tomorrow."

I could have done cartwheels. Seth was going to call me! We might go out again . . . twice in one weekend!

With admirable self-restraint I said good night, got out of the car, and strolled into the building. Inside, though, when I knew he couldn't see me, I hugged myself and spun around in an ecstatic circle.

My lips were still burning from Seth's kisses as I started typing in my diary a few minutes later. *"I'm describing this for posterity: my first date with Seth Modine!"* I typed in the names of the other people who'd been at Fiona's. *"To be honest, the party was a little on the dull side. But I am not complaining. Being with Seth was totally amazing. I sort of feel like I'm putting on an act when I*

*crack those cynical jokes and with the black clothes
and all, but . . ."* I touched my lips with my fingertips. *"Those kisses were for real."*

I turned off my computer. I figured I'd try to go
to sleep. Not that I needed to dream. My dreams
had come true already.

Six

Winter thawed into early spring, and there was a picture of Seth Modine in my birthday locket. We were going out, and I was popular in a way I'd never been before. I got invited to parties every weekend—I was the It girl of the moment. I was too busy to feel lonely about being the only sister left at home anymore. I was too busy for a lot of things, like homework.

"And like your old friends," Noelle said one night over the phone.

It was the week before the talent show, and I'd been rehearsing my poem in my bedroom. "What are you talking about?"

She sighed. "I don't want to whine, Lil. Mickey and I are just sad, that's all. We thought we were your best friends, but we never see you anymore."

"Don't be ridiculous," I said. "You *are* my best friends. That hasn't changed. Don't I always get you invited to the parties I'm going to?"

"You get us invited, but that doesn't mean we're welcome," Noelle said.

I knew she had a point. Either you were It or you weren't, and their friendship with me wasn't

73

quite enough to make Noelle and Mickey It. They just weren't intellectual enough. But I still liked them, of course.

"We'll do something together soon, just the three of us, okay?" I promised.

"How about this weekend? Maybe Saturday?"

"Talent show," I reminded her. "There's a party at Rico's afterward. I'll make sure you're on the list."

"Okay, Lil. Thanks. Well . . . later."

"Later!"

My telephone rings at least five times a night these days—Hal finally sprang for a second line out of desperation. As soon as I hung up with Noelle, Loryn called. Then Seth. The call after that was from Daniel.

"Hi!" I said with genuine pleasure. For a while he and I had been talking on the phone or getting together once or twice a week. Lately I hadn't heard from him. "What's up, pardner?"

"Uh, is this okay?" he asked.

"Is what okay?"

"You know, calling you. Should I still do this now that you have a, you know, boyfriend?"

I really didn't see any connection between having a boyfriend and talking to Daniel about writing. There'd been that time he almost asked me out—if that had even been his intention—but that was ancient history now. "Sure," I said. "Of course you should call. Seth wouldn't mind, if that's what you mean. Why would he?"

"No reason," Daniel said. "So, what are you writing about for the next assignment?"

I was kind of in a rut in writing class. All my stories sounded the same, and every time I got a paper back, Mrs. Cobb's comments sounded the same, too. But I wasn't worried about it. Seth and I were in sync. Why would I obsess about the fact that I'd never clicked with Mrs. Cobb?

"I'm writing a sequel to my piece for the talent show," I told Daniel. "A longer piece, not a poem this time. Listen."

I told him my idea. As usual he wasn't wild about it, and as usual I didn't care. When we hung up, I tried to do some writing. The sequel just wasn't happening, so I turned to a clean page of narrow-ruled paper.

I looked over at the picture of my father. Suddenly I had a strong impulse. I never write about Dad, I thought. There were so many stories I could tell about him! But who'd want to hear them?

Instead I made an entry in my journal. *"I gotta admit it's getting to be a strain, churning out these stories for class,"* I typed. *"It's a relief to write in my diary and use capitals and punctuation. 'Then try something else for a change,' Daniel would say. Hey, you don't mess with success."*

I turned off my computer and went over to the window. It was almost April, and a gentle spring rain tapped against the panes. April showers bring May flowers, I thought. And what did Daisy used to say? She had her own rhyme—something about opening day in the major leagues.

Cupping my chin in my hands, I propped my elbows on the windowsill and tried to remember Daisy's rhyme. I couldn't. A weird longing came over me. "Why couldn't she speak to me one more time?" I whispered.

Turning from the window, I went to my bookshelf and pulled out my Daisy photo album. I hadn't looked through it in a while. I hadn't visited the cemetery recently, either. It seemed childish, somehow—having conversations with my sister's gravestone. I would've died of embarrassment if anyone had ever seen me.

Now I looked at my photos of Daisy. There she was, shooting a goal during a soccer game, posing with Kristin and Jamila in their South Regional High graduation gowns, on a toboggan with me and Laurel, popping a wheelie on her bike, blowing out the candles on her birthday cake at her sweet-sixteen clambake.

"You wouldn't believe how great my life has been since *I* turned sixteen," I told her. "You should see me, Daze. I used to be an oddball, remember? Not anymore."

My sister smiled out of the graduation photograph. I squinted, trying to see into those eyes. Usually I felt some kind of bond, but it wasn't there tonight.

In fact, I didn't feel anything at all.

*   *   *

Rose and Stephen came home the first weekend in April so they could go to my talent show on Saturday night and then to a coed bridal shower for Rose's old friend Cath Appleby and her fiancé on Sunday morning. When they got in around five on Friday, I greeted Rose at the door with a Euro-style cheek-to-cheek air kiss. "No hug?" she asked.

I raised an ironic eyebrow. "Do we need to be so sentimental?"

Rose grabbed me, anyway. No sooner had she pulled me close, though, than she pushed me away again. "What's with the specs?" she asked.

"I need glasses," I said. It wasn't *really* a lie—I did need them. For my image.

"Since when?"

"Since recently."

"Oh," she said, still looking puzzled.

She and Stephen had arrived in time for dinner. Hal brought home Chinese food—he likes to give Mom a break from cooking now and then. "I'm so psyched Cath's getting married," Rose said, dipping her mini–spring roll into sweet-and-sour sauce and then popping it into her mouth. She chewed and swallowed. "Now I won't be the only one in our old crowd who's settled down." She nudged Stephen with her elbow. "You know, tied to the old ball and chain."

"Gee, thanks," he said.

"Is anyone going to eat that last spring roll?" Rose asked, reaching for the carton. "Because if not . . ."

"Help yourself," Hal said, even though she already had.

"Hey, whatever happened with the Broadway show?" I asked.

Rose put up a hand in a just-a-minute sign so she could finish chewing . "I didn't get a part," she said a minute later.

"That's too bad," I commiserated.

"I'm sorry, Rose," Mom said. "You must be disappointed."

"Yeah, but it's for the best." Rose certainly didn't *look* disappointed—she had a huge grin on her face. "I'm not too bummed about it because . . . I'm going to have a baby. I'm pregnant!"

For a moment nobody spoke. Then Mom jumped out of her chair with a delighted shriek. She and Rose hugged, talking a mile a minute. "Just barely pregnant," Rose told Mom. "I'm not due until November."

"Are you having morning sickness?" Mom asked.

Rose shook her head. "No. I'm hungry all the time, though."

Mom laughed. "I noticed. Oh, Hal, can you believe it? We're going to be grandparents!"

Rose turned to me. "And you're going to be an aunt, Lil. Aren't you excited?"

I *was* excited, but I wasn't about to start jumping up and down like an idiot. Wearing black all the time makes a person a lot less demonstrative—it just goes with the territory. "Sure," I said casually.

My underwhelmed response didn't really matter because everyone else was so enthusiastic. Rose called Laurel to tell her the news, and we could hear Laurel exclaiming on the other end of the phone. Laurel was still at U. Maine—she hadn't been able to get away for the talent show because she had a big chemistry test coming up the next week.

When she hung up after speaking with Laurel, Rose was smiling. A second later her eyes brimmed with tears. "I really wish I could share this with Daisy, too," she said.

Mom and Rose embraced again. I felt an ache under my ribs. But I didn't cry or join the hug fest. I don't know; I just couldn't get into the Hallmark moment. I wondered what Seth would have thought of the whole scene.

The next day Stephen took his law school books over to the town library for a couple of hours. Mom and Rose discussed layettes and nursery decor. I hung out with them, figuring that listening to baby talk beat stressing over the talent show, which started in just a few hours.

"What do you think about a stenciled border of yellow ducks and blue sailboats on the wall," Rose asked Mom, "and a yellow-and-white-striped crib bumper?"

"Cute," Mom said. "You'll have to take the old rocking chair, Rose. It's the one I rocked in with you girls when you were infants."

"How about names?" I asked.

"We're thinking about David for a boy and Jane for a girl," Rose told me.

"Jane?" I wrinkled my nose. "That's so boring."

Rose laughed. "What names do you like?"

"How about Bianca?" I suggested. "Or Victoria?"

Rose lifted her eyes skyward. "Why did I ask?"

"All right, are you girls ready for a project?" Mom got to her feet. "Come up to the attic with me."

The three of us went upstairs. Mom pulled down the folding ladder in the hall ceiling and we took turns climbing up it. "What are we looking for?" Rose asked once we were standing in the attic.

"There's a trunk here somewhere with old baby things, Rose," Mom said. "You girls all wore a beautiful hand-embroidered christening dress that my grandmother made when my mother was a baby. Let's see if we can find it."

The attic was musty and cluttered. I shifted some boxes to get at a beat-up old trunk, coughing at the dust I'd kicked up. Meanwhile Mom lifted the latch on another old trunk. "What's in here?" Rose asked.

Mom pulled out a cardboard shoe box. "Old family papers and photographs. I keep meaning to come up here some rainy day and sort through it all, but I never get around to it."

Rose and I went over to take a look. "What gorgeous curls," Rose said, pointing to a sepia-tinted photograph of a child in an old-fashioned pinafore.

"Who's that little girl?" I asked.

Mom turned the photo over and laughed. "It's a little boy," she said. "Your dad's grandpa Simon."

"Why'd they put him in a dress?" I wondered.

"That was the style back then," Rose said.

"Look at this one," Mom said. "Do you recognize *that* little boy?"

In the faded color snapshot a man in a water-proof slicker and boots stood on the deck of a fishing boat with his hand resting proudly on the head of a freckle-faced boy. The boy was holding a bucket full of cod and grinning. He was missing a front tooth. "It's Dad," I said, "with Great-uncle Ted."

"Can I have that?" Rose asked. "I'd like to put it in a frame."

"Of course," Mom said. Rose took the picture, handling it carefully. "Let's see if we can find some others as good for Laurel and Lily to take."

Mom opened another shoe box. Inside it were small, leather-bound books. She lifted one up. "It's a diary," she said.

I stepped closer, curious. "Whose?"

She turned to the first page. "'This diary is the exclusive and very private property of Flora Elizabeth White,'" Mom read, "'and is not to be perused by strange eyes on penalty of death.'" Mom smiled. "Sound familiar, Lily?"

I used to label my own journal notebooks with dire warnings like that. "Maybe we shouldn't read this, then," I said.

Mom laughed. "Oh, I think it's okay. Flora

Elizabeth White grew up to be your great-grandmother Flora Walker. She's been dead for twenty years."

"Great-grandma Flora—the one with the charm bracelet?" I asked.

Mom nodded. "That's right."

"She was pretty prolific," Rose observed. "Look at all these volumes."

"I didn't realize she was a writer." Mom looked at me. "I bet you'd enjoy reading them, Lily. Maybe they'd give you some ideas for stories."

I shrugged. I was kind of curious about the diaries but didn't want to show it. As I've said, enthusiasm wasn't a virtue in the crowd I was currently hanging with. "I'm sure it's mostly pretty boring," I said in a disinterested manner.

Mom put the box aside. "Let's bring them downstairs, anyway."

We continued hunting for the baby stuff. Rose opened up a trunk. "Dress-up clothes," she said as she sifted through the things. "Remember this ratty old velvet cape, Lil? And these cardboard swords decorated with plastic jewels?"

"For playing The Three Musketeers," I said.

Mom laughed. "Remember when Lily wore her D'Artagnan costume for a week straight and the only thing we could get her to say was, 'All for one and one for all'?"

"Here's another Lily special," Rose said, digging out a moth-eaten mouse costume.

"That was another one you kept on for a

week," Mom recalled, "and ate nothing but cheese the whole time."

"I'd change the ears sometimes," I said, "and the tail. I could be a rabbit or a horse or an elephant."

"You were wild," Rose concluded. "We never knew *what* to expect from you."

Rose sounded nostalgic for the old days, and suddenly I felt nostalgic, too. It was fun having a personality that changed all the time, I thought somewhat wistfully. I looked down at the clothes I was wearing now—black jeans and a black T-shirt—and for a second I felt trapped. My current look and attitude didn't leave me much room to grow.

"Here are the baby outfits," Mom announced.

She and Rose began to ooh and ah over tiny sweaters and crocheted booties. I closed the lid of the costume trunk. No more make-believe, I decided.

I'd found the real me at last.

were," Mario recalled, "and watching the others of the world stop.

"'I desire the cup magazine.' I smile," said the girl. Perilla, a goddess who knows no time or sex or place.

"'You were with Dioia Chignazel,' my master knew what to expect each day..."

For a second I hesitate for the sad days, and suddenly I felt noticeable and it was the day, as the moment that I forget of the time, I thought something ahead of I was a friend and a fellow. I was wearing now—black pants and a black T-shirt—and very natural I felt impelled a portrait I, for example, didn't make a single item to sew.

"Here are the baby clothes. At ten tomorrow she will be in space so you will all asleep now sweet as any of us and spoke I placed the lid of the machine which, as I now understand believe, I distanced.

And I found the final step at last.

Seven

Or had I?

Mom, Rose, Stephen, and Hal came to the talent show that night. Afterward in the crowded, noisy hall outside the high school auditorium, they showered me with hugs. "You were great!" Rose exclaimed.

"A riot," Stephen agreed.

"It went okay, didn't it?" I asked, trying not to grin from ear to ear.

"The audience laughed like crazy," Hal said.

"Yep, you're ready for off Broadway," Rose concluded.

Mom was the only one who hadn't spoken up. "What did *you* think, Mom?" I asked.

"The poem was definitely . . . interesting. Surprising." She smiled wryly. "I must just be an out-of-touch old lady."

"You didn't get it?" I said.

She shook her head. "Well, I sort of got it. It was about a girl who couldn't find a date for the prom, who didn't fit in at school. She was practically suicidal. Yet it was supposed to be . . ."

"Funny," I supplied. "You know, ironic. It's black humor, Mom."

"Well, anyway, I'm proud of you." Mom gave me another hug. "And we're taking you out for dessert to celebrate."

We went to the Harborside. Seth came along. It was the first time Rose had met my new boyfriend, and for me this was almost as important as performing in the talent show. I wanted her to approve of him. But for some reason, they didn't hit it off. It was sort of like Mom and my poem. Rose just didn't seem to get Seth.

I knew it for sure halfway through my cheesecake. Seth kept making fun of kids who'd performed in the talent show, and in a playful way Rose challenged pretty much every remark he made. He didn't let up, though, and finally Rose just said, "Hmmm," while Stephen stuffed a huge bite of lemon meringue pie into his mouth to hide his smile. They think Seth's full of it, I realized.

Suddenly I was dying to get out of there. I pushed my plate away and refolded my cloth napkin, then stood up. "Seth and I are going to a party at Rico's," I told Mom. "Can I stay out a little later than usual? You know, to celebrate?"

Mom glanced at Hal. He shrugged. "Sure," she decided. "You can stay out until one."

"Thanks." I bent over to kiss Mom's cheek. "See you all tomorrow."

Seth and I made our getaway, leaving the others

to finish their coffee. "I like Rose," Seth said as we drove to Rico's. "She's cool."

"Yeah." I found myself telling a bald-faced lie. I didn't want to hurt his feelings. "She liked you, too."

Seth slipped an arm around my shoulders and smiled an of-course-she-did smile. I couldn't quite smile back, so I turned my head away to look out the window. Seth *is* full of it, I thought. I don't blame Rose. He really came off as a pompous jerk.

I was about to tell him he could be a little more charitable toward kids who'd had the nerve to get up onstage in front of hundreds of people when he abruptly pulled the car over to the side of the road. I glanced at him, startled, and he put his arms around me and kissed me on the mouth. "You were phenomenal tonight, Lily," he murmured. His lips explored my jaw and then my throat. "I can't believe you're mine."

After that I mellowed out. Why pick a fight? I decided. Seth thought I was phenomenal, and that summed up my feelings for him, too.

Our impromptu make-out session made us fashionably late for Rico's party. It was big—fifty or more people. Half an hour into the party, though, it occurred to me that there were quite a few faces missing. "I thought Rico invited everyone who was in the talent show," I said to Seth and Loryn as we cracked open our sodas. "Where are Ginny Lauer and Andrew Hunt?"

Loryn laughed. "Are you *kidding?*"

"No," I said. Out of the corner of my eye I spotted Mickey and Noelle. They looked like they were getting up their nerve to approach a group of people, including Fiona and Rico. "And those AV guys who did the lights—Izzy and Clay?"

"They didn't make the final cut," Seth said.

I looked at him, my head tilted to one side. "What final cut?"

"Rico wanted to keep the party exclusive," he explained.

"You mean Rico didn't even invite them?" I asked. I could see Noelle and Mickey being squeezed out of Rico and Fiona's circle.

Loryn rolled her eyes. "Of course not!"

"But this is supposed to be the official talent show cast party," I said. "It's not really fair to leave people out."

"You were going to spend the evening getting to know Izzy and Clay?" Seth teased. "Yeah, they seem like true Renaissance men."

"We knew they wouldn't come," Loryn said to me.

"So we just made an executive decision," Seth finished.

"I still think you should've invited them," I said crossly.

Seth put an arm around my waist. "This is really touching, Lily," he joked. "I didn't know you harbored such tender feelings for your fellow man."

Have a sense of humor, I told myself, but tonight I didn't feel like laughing at someone else's expense. Everyone in the talent show had worked equally hard. So what if Clay, Izzy, Ginny, and Andrew weren't the coolest kids in Hawk Harbor?

I wiggled free of Seth's embrace. "Be right back," I muttered. "I need to find someone."

I hadn't had a minute to talk to Noelle and Mickey yet, and by the time I caught up with them, they were putting on their jackets and heading for the door. "Where are you going?" I asked.

"Walk us out to my car," Noelle invited.

When we were outside, I said, "What's up, guys?"

"We're heading over to my house to watch cable," Noelle said.

I didn't really have to ask, but I did, anyway. "Aren't you having fun?"

Noelle laughed. "Lil, it was great to see you in the talent show. We're really proud of you. But these parties . . . no one talks to us."

"Well, come back in and hang with me and Seth. I'm sure people will talk to you if you give them a chance," I urged.

Mickey shot Noelle a sideways glance. "No, thanks," she said.

I felt hurt, and I guess I looked hurt, too. "No offense, Lil," Noelle assured me. "We still love you."

"But when you're with that crowd, you're not yourself," Mickey said. "We don't really feel welcome."

"Hey, don't try to spare my feelings," I said sarcastically. "Tell it like it is."

Mickey bit her lip. "I'm sorry, Lil, but that's how it feels on this end."

"Well, you *are* welcome to join us, but it's your choice, obviously." I crossed my arms across my chest.

"See you around," Noelle said, and she and Mickey climbed into the car.

I turned on my heel and stormed back to the party. They're so high maintenance, I fumed. Why do I even bother? But I knew that was the point. I hadn't been bothering for a while. Seth's friends *weren't* Mickey and Noelle's friends, and since I'd started going out with Seth, I'd shut my old friends out of my life. Now I was paying the price. *They* were blowing *me* off.

Once I was back inside, everything felt normal again. People bugged me until I recited my poem from the talent show one more time. When Rico got out his camera, we all posed for pictures, Seth and I with our arms wrapped around each other, and even though I'd been kind of mad at him before, now I pressed my cheek against his and thought, This one will be in the yearbook. Coolest junior class couple.

At 1 A.M. Seth drove me home, where we shared a final, passionate good-bye kiss. In the apartment I tiptoed upstairs. Everything was dark and quiet. After washing up and getting into my nightgown, I turned on my laptop and started typing.

It was a relief to be curled up in bed, alone with my diary. *"Rose wasn't too impressed by Seth,"* I wrote in my journal. *"The whole time at the Harborside she was either yawning or being confrontational. Maybe she was just tired,"* I added hopefully. *"Pregnant women are always tired, right?"*

I decided this was the best explanation for Rose's behavior. But it didn't necessarily explain Seth. *"We had a fight at Rico's,"* I typed. *"Well, not really a fight. We didn't see eye to eye about something. It wasn't a big deal, though. I'm over it."*

I paused, staring at the sentence I'd just written. Was I, though? Over it?

I turned off my computer. I didn't want to write in my journal anymore. I didn't want to ask questions that didn't have easy answers.

So I didn't write this question down, but as I turned out the light and tried to fall asleep, it buzzed in my brain, anyway. If this is the real me at last, why is it suddenly such hard work to be Lily Walker?

It was May, and the school year was almost over. "I can't believe the prom is this weekend!" Noelle exclaimed one Wednesday in the cafeteria.

I'd barely spoken to Mickey and Noelle since

that scene at Rico's party, but today was Mickey's birthday, so we were celebrating. Well, *they* were celebrating. I was moping. "I know," I said, licking frosting off one of the cupcakes Noelle had brought. "And Seth's home sick with a stomach flu."

"He'll be back on his feet by Saturday," Mickey predicted.

"He'd better be," I said.

But he wasn't. In fact, his stomach flu turned out not to be stomach flu at all—Seth ended up in the community hospital having his appendix removed. I went stag to my first prom, sharing a limo with Loryn and Fiona and their dates, Dylan and Brett.

"Poor Seth," Fiona said, slouching elegantly in her seat. She was wearing a slinky midnight blue strapless dress with chunky high heels.

"It's a major bummer," Brett agreed, adjusting his bow tie.

I was wearing a black slip dress and my birthday necklace with the charm from my great-grandmother's bracelet. Now I took the necklace off and opened the book-shaped locket so I could see the little picture of my boyfriend inside.

"Look," I said with a sigh, showing it to Loryn.

"Even when he's not with us, we somehow feel his presence," she joked in a preacherly tone.

I took the locket back. Seth gazed up at me. He had a half smile on his face, and his eyes were narrowed. He was sticking his chin out a little. He always does that in pictures, I thought now for the first time. That kind of rugged, cool chin thing. I frowned. He looks like a model. A little too posed.

I closed the locket quickly. I shouldn't be having such mean thoughts about my poor sick boyfriend. "I took him his boutonniere in the hospital," I told Loryn and the others. I didn't tell them that Seth had acted like he couldn't have cared less about the whole thing.

Plenty of kids were at the dance without dates, so even though I missed Seth, I wasn't a wallflower. I got asked to dance a lot, and by some really cool guys. Seth's buddy Bob Sokolov came over to me just as the band kicked into a particularly excellent song. We started dancing, and he wasn't bad. He also had a very cool tux, complete with collarless shirt. But he spent the entire time looking everywhere but at my face, as if he were checking the crowd to see who might be watching us. It was a bore.

When the song ended, I politely asked him if he wanted to dance another one, praying he'd say no. Lucky for me he was ready to hit the refreshment table. I took another route to the same destination, bumping into Daniel on the way. "Hey," I said, a wide smile spreading across my face.

"Hey, yourself," he replied, grinning back at me.

He handed me a cup of punch and then took one for himself. "Who are you here with?" I asked.

"I'm flying solo," he answered.

I realized I didn't know much about Daniel's social life, even though we'd become buddies in writing class. "You procrastinated too long and Princess Charming said yes to someone else?" I kidded.

"Something like that." He looked down into his punch cup. "How about you? Where's Mr. Modine?"

I told Daniel about Seth's appendectomy. "Ouch," Daniel said, wincing. "Bad timing, huh?"

"Actually, he didn't seem that torn up about missing the prom," I told Daniel. "He thinks the whole concept is totally bourgeois."

We finished our punch and tossed our cups in the trash. "Want to dance?" I asked.

Daniel lifted his hands palms outward in a "no, no, not me, never" gesture. "Two left feet," he explained. "*Three* left feet."

I laughed. "It's the *prom*, Daniel. You have to dance with somebody."

"Well . . ." He smoothed his hair back self-consciously.

I grabbed his arm. "Come on!"

We danced a couple of fast songs. Daniel actually had some nice moves. He was relaxed and limber, not totally stiff like a lot of guys. "You're a great dancer," I told him, shaking my head. "I can't believe you tried to feed me that stuff about left feet."

Daniel shrugged. I lifted my shoulders, too. We

started moving our shoulders back and forth in rhythm, which made me laugh. "You make it work," he said. "I have two left feet and you have two right ones."

Whatever it was, we melded pretty well. Daniel was a decent slow dancer, too. When the music changed, he hesitated for a split second before taking me in his arms, but then he didn't wimp out. He didn't hold me at a distance, like we were waltzing in sixth-grade ballroom dance class—he pulled me close and moved with me in a self-assured way.

"I can't believe you don't have a date," I told him, surprising myself.

Daniel raised his eyebrows. Two red spots popped up on his cheeks. "Truth *is* stranger than fiction."

"No, seriously. You're so sweet!" I patted his lapel. "*And* you look okay in formal wear. There are so many girls at school who didn't get asked to the prom and who would've been totally psyched to go with you. You should've done someone a big favor."

"But then I wouldn't be available to substitute for hospitalized boyfriends, would I?" he pointed out.

"True."

I *was* selfishly glad that Daniel didn't have to run off and pay attention to another girl. It was tons more fun dancing with him than with a guy like Bob. Daniel was actually interested in me, not in how he looked dancing with me.

"Isn't it great that Mrs. Cobb decided not to give a final?" Daniel asked.

We were still slow dancing. "Yeah," I agreed as we swayed back and forth. "Although I wouldn't have minded a chance to pull my grade up a little. Looks like I'll be getting a B."

"That's not so bad."

There didn't seem much point in telling him about how high my hopes for the class had been back in January. "Mrs. Cobb just never warmed to my writing."

Daniel tried some Fred Astaire stuff—he lifted my right hand in the air, then placed his other hand on the small of my back and spun me neatly under his arm. "What about next year?"

Mrs. Cobb had just announced that she'd be teaching a continuation of the creative-writing class next semester. This time people would have to try out for a limited number of spaces by submitting a manuscript over the summer. "It sounds pretty intense," I said.

"I think I'll take a shot at it, anyway. You should, too, Lily."

I shrugged. "Who knows? Fall's a long way off."

We were quiet for a minute. I tuned in to the music, which was lush and hypnotic. With a contented sigh I rested my head on Daniel's shoulder.

An instant later I jumped back. "Oops!" I said. Now I was the one with pink cheeks. "Forgot where I was for a minute there."

"It's okay," Daniel said softly.

I looked into his eyes. Next thing I knew, the song was over, and Loryn and Fiona and their dates swooped down on me, and the whole pack of us were dancing, and Daniel had disappeared. I guess it was a good thing that the song had ended when it did. I *had* almost forgotten something. It was so easy to be with Daniel and so much fun, I'd almost forgotten that he wasn't my prom date.

Eight

Summer vacation started one week before Memorial Day. "I need to look for a job, don't I?" I asked Mom and Hal one night as we ate a picnic supper in the park down the block.

When they turned sixteen, my older sisters had all gotten jobs to start saving money for college. Daisy's first real summer job had been at the hospital (where Seth had his appendectomy)—she had worked as a receptionist. That's what sparked her interest in studying medicine. Even though she'd taken a year off in between high school and college to work full-time and help out the family, she'd never lost sight of her goal. She'd been totally dedicated and focused.

"Might not be a bad idea," Mom said, scooping some pasta salad onto a plastic plate and handing it to me.

"You know what I'd really like to do," I told her. "Work for you at Potluck."

The gourmet shop's grand opening was scheduled for Memorial Day weekend, when tourism season starts in earnest in Hawk Harbor. Mom opened a Tupperware container and nibbled a strawberry. "I remember you mentioning that. It's a possibility."

I pictured myself behind the counter at Potluck, hobnobbing with wealthy summer people who came in looking for basil-infused olive oil or goose liver pâté. "I'll wait on customers. I have good people skills."

"I think if you work at the store, you should start in the kitchen, helping Sarah," Mom commented.

"You mean Laurel gets to be assistant manager and I get to chop carrots?" I asked in an offended tone.

"Laurel's an adult now," Mom said, unruffled. "She's ready for the responsibility—she has some experience under her belt."

"Taking care of mangy wild animals," I mumbled. "Are you sure you want her handling food?"

I couldn't change Mom's mind, though. I could be a prep cook at Potluck, working behind the scenes—she reminded me that Laurel had done that sort of work for her off and on for the last couple of years—or I could look for another job. I decided to accept her offer, even if it did mean having to play second fiddle to my older sister.

Laurel was home from college for the summer, but Carlos had a summer job a couple of hours away in a lab at Tufts University, near Boston. Laurel was brooding like crazy.

Despite that, it was nice having a sister at home again. She'd taken over her old bedroom, and already it had that familiar zoolike odor, thanks to Snickers the dog, two birds, and a mini–lop-eared rabbit named Ebenezer. Animals are not my thing, but I could put up with them if it meant having Laurel around. It was nice having someone to talk to.

One Friday after dinner Laurel, Mom, and Hal sat down at the kitchen table to go over lists of things they needed to do before Potluck's grand opening. I lurked nearby, hoping someone would ask for my opinion.

"You seem distracted," Mom said to Laurel. "You know, I don't want to ruin your summer. If you think being assistant manager will put too much pressure on you, we can change your job description a little."

"It won't be any pressure at all compared to school," Laurel said, sticking her hands into the pockets of her overalls and slouching in her chair. "I guess I should just put it behind me, you know? Start fresh next fall. But I keep thinking about how I blew my math final."

"You didn't blow it," Hal said.

"I got a C," Laurel insisted, "and it pulled my semester grade down to a B."

"I think you should be proud of yourself," Mom declared. "Your second-semester grades were better than your first-semester ones. Next year you'll do even better."

"Next year. Huh," Laurel huffed. "I'll tell you one thing about next year. I'm dropping out of the prevet program. Everyone in those classes is super-competitive. I hate it."

Mom put the Potluck papers aside, and she, Laurel, and Hal continued talking about Laurel's academic career. I wandered off, drinking my iced tea thoughtfully. Nature Girl was having an identity crisis. Interesting!

Later I barged into her room without knocking, the way I always do. "Are you really going to drop prevet?" I asked, flopping onto her bed.

Laurel was sitting at her desk, writing a letter—to Carlos, I guessed.

She turned in her chair to look at me. "Yeah, I am," she said. "I mean, I hope I don't sound like a baby, whining because I didn't get straight A's, but I busted my butt all year and I feel like I don't have anything to show for it. I might still major in bio, but at least I won't have to take so many other hard-core science classes."

I wondered what Daisy would have said at a moment like this. She'd been the family cheerleader. "What about your furry and feathered friends?" I gestured at Laurel's menagerie. "You owe it to them to become a vet. You *love* animals. I used to think you *were* an animal."

"I can still have pets," Laurel pointed out.

"Okay, so what about Carlos?"

"What *about* Carlos?"

"I thought you guys were going to have related careers, like when you used to work at the Wildlife Rescue Center."

Laurel tapped her pen on the desk, frowning. "I don't know anymore. He graduated magna cum laude—he's going to Tufts for grad school. How can I compete with that? Maybe I'm not smart enough—maybe we don't belong together."

"That's the most ridiculous thing I ever heard," I declared. "You *are* smart, and you and Carlos are perfect for each other. It shouldn't make a difference if you don't both end up going to graduate school. Anyway, you still might. It's a couple of years away."

"You're right." Laurel turned back to her letter. "Who knows what will happen?"

This conversation struck me as so odd that I couldn't get it out of my mind. The next morning Rose came up to Hawk Harbor for the day—Stephen had just finished his second year of law school, and he had an orientation for his summer job at a firm in Boston—and I felt I had to talk with her about Laurel.

"You should give her some advice," I told Rose. "She'd listen to you because you actually have real-life experience."

Rose heaved a sigh. We were sitting on the family room couch, watching the Saturday morning cooking shows on public TV, and she was resting her folded arms on top of her stomach, which was starting to stick out. "How can *I* give her advice? It's not like I have it all figured out or anything."

"Are you kidding?" I said. "You're the most together person I know."

To my surprise, instead of being flattered, Rose burst into tears. "Are you okay?" I asked worriedly. "Are you nauseated or something?"

"I'm not nauseated," Rose blubbered, "but I'm not okay, either."

"Well, what's wrong?"

"I just don't know if I'm ready to have a baby, Lil. What if I don't know how to take care of it? What if my career is sidetracked forever? What if I'm a t-terrible m-mom?"

I patted my sister's shoulder while she sobbed noisily for a minute. "You'll be a great mom, Rose, and your career *won't* get sidetracked," I said with certainty. "There are lots of singers and actresses out there with babies and stuff, and it doesn't slow them down one bit."

Rose sniffled. "Like who?"

"Like Madonna," I said, "and Uma Thurman and Jodie Foster. And there are athletes and supermodels who have babies and then go back to work, too. Everybody does it these days."

Rose wiped her eyes on the sleeve of her maternity T-shirt. "Don't think I'm crazy, okay? It's just the hormones. I'm extremely volatile lately."

"What can I do to make you feel better?" I asked.

She gave me a wry smile. "How about a glass of milk and some Pop-tarts?"

"*My sisters are wacko these days,*" I typed in my journal an hour later. "*We're talking certifiable. Like, they have really great lives: Laurel's a freshman at a good university with a totally gorgeous, devoted boyfriend, and Rose has a cool career and a great husband* plus *she's expecting a baby. But for some reason they're both freaking out about stuff and having all this self-doubt. I don't get it."*

I stopped writing and looked pensively out the window. The trees lining Main Street were lush and green, and in the distance the peaceful blue harbor was spotted with sailboats. How can Laurel just suddenly decide that she doesn't want to be a vet? I wondered. When she's wanted to be one all her life? It was totally confusing. And Rose, talking about quitting her singing career to stay home with the baby. What was *that* all about?

My sisters aren't done growing up, I realized. It was a revelation. I'd just assumed that by the time people graduated from high school or at least college, they were done with that kind of stuff. Apparently not.

I'd always taken Daisy for my model. She knew exactly who she was and what she wanted to do with every hour in every day, for the rest of her life. *"But maybe it's not always that easy. Maybe for some people identity is a learning process,"* I typed in my journal. *"Rose and Laurel are still figuring out who they are."*

I hit the return key and started a new paragraph. *"And if they're still figuring out who they are . . . then what about me?"*

Nine

Suddenly it was the official beginning of summer and Mom was in a total panic.

"Relax," Stephen said, pouring Mom a glass of wine. He and Rose were home for Memorial Day weekend. Carlos was visiting, too—everyone wanted to be on hand for Potluck's grand opening the next day. Rose had made dinner, and we'd forced Mom to sit down at the table with us. "You and Hal are the most organized people on the planet," Stephen went on. "You've thought of everything—it'll go great."

"I don't know." Mom chewed her lip anxiously. Hal pushed her wineglass closer to her, but Mom didn't touch it. "What if no one comes to the store? Or what if they just browse and don't buy anything?"

"You did tons of market research," Rose reminded Mom as she set a platter of broiled halibut on the table. "There's no other store like it for miles."

"I just don't know," Mom repeated. She toyed with her silverware, straightening the knife and spoon until they were precisely parallel. "I was up half the night, looking at the numbers again." She shot a glance at Hal. "We've really stretched ourselves to finance this. What if Potluck flops?"

Hal gave Mom a hug. "If it flops, we'll start over—you've done it before. But it *won't* flop," he said. "I guarantee you're going to be so busy tomorrow, your head will be spinning."

We started eating. "Great fish, Rose," Carlos said. Laurel's boyfriend has short black hair and dark eyes and a killer smile, but he's a man of few words. If he said the fish was great, you better believe it was.

"Thanks." Rose was already serving herself seconds. She was eating like a horse. Make that a team of horses. The big kind. "Anyone else want more?"

We passed the fish and side dishes around the table. I scooped a little more rice pilaf onto my plate.

"I was biking down Lighthouse Road earlier," Laurel said, taking a platter from me. "The Lilac Inn is still for sale."

"Supposedly they had an offer a month or so ago, but the deal fell through," Hal said.

Rose looked at Mom. "You and Hal are thinking about buying a house, aren't you?"

Laurel's eyes lit up. "Wouldn't it be fun to live there again?"

"They're not asking a bad price, either," Stephen put in.

Rose glanced at Stephen. "How do *you* know?"

"I called the realtor," he confessed, shrugging. "Just curious."

"Let's do it, then!" I exclaimed. "Let's buy our old house back!"

Mom shook her head, laughing. "You kids are too much," she said. "It wouldn't be the right house for me and Hal even if we had the money right now. Three floors and six bedrooms! Not exactly practical, with only one of you girls at home."

I heaved a dramatic sigh. "Dreams don't come true if you're always being *practical*," I said.

Mom smiled again. "Be that as it may."

"So, we have a present for you, Mom." Rose hopped to her feet and went over to the sideboard, retrieving a large, flat, gift-wrapped box. "Here."

"What is it?" Mom asked.

"Open it," Rose said, smiling.

Mom ripped off the paper and opened the box. She lifted out something and started to unfold it. "What . . . ?"

She held it up. It was a green twill apron with the word *Potluck* embroidered on it in bright yellow. "Look at this," Mom said. "It's adorable!"

"There's one for each of us," Laurel explained.

"We picked the colors to match the sign and the menus," I contributed.

"It's the perfect touch," Mom said. "You girls are so thoughtful. These aprons make having my own store seem real."

"It's real, all right," Rose agreed.

After dinner Rose and Stephen went out with

some old high school friends. Laurel and I cleaned up the kitchen while Mom and Hal took turns making phone calls to people Mom had catered for, reminding them to come to the grand opening. "Are *you* nervous?" I asked Laurel as I rinsed a plate and stuck it in the dishwasher.

Laurel's always been kind of shy. "You know me," Laurel replied, putting a platter in the sink and squirting dishwashing liquid onto it. "I'd rather be behind the scenes. But I'm flattered that Mom thinks I can contribute something." Laurel cracked a smile. "Her mistake, right?"

"It's not a mistake," I surprised myself by saying. I'd been about to launch into a complaint about how unfair it was that Laurel had a job that I'd be a hundred times better at. Instead I decided to try to make my big sister feel good about herself. She *should* feel good. "You're really smart and reliable. And you'll look good in the apron," I added, "because it's green . . . Nature Girl."

We both laughed.

Saturday morning before Memorial Day the excitement was at a fever pitch in the new store. Laurel and I ran around, scrambling to help customers and keep the shelves stocked. Rose stayed for the day, too, helping the cooks and popping out of the kitchen frequently to talk to people she knew. The store was packed with customers all day long. I tried to keep track of how much stuff we were selling—half a dozen bottles of raspberry vinegar, pounds and pounds of Mom's fresh salads, cooking utensils, gourmet salsas and chutneys in pretty jars, fresh-baked scones and brownies, dish towels, cookbooks—but after a couple of hours I lost track. All I knew was that we didn't have a quiet moment, and when six o'clock came, there were still people in the store, so we stayed open an extra twenty minutes.

When the front door was finally shut and locked, Sarah started cleaning up the kitchen, and the rest of us collapsed out front. Rose literally lay down flat on her back on the rug.

"What a day!" Laurel said.

Hitting a few buttons on the computerized cash register, Hal came up with the grand total of the day's receipts. When he said the number out loud, we all screeched.

"Are we going to be rich, rich, rich beyond our wildest dreams?" I asked my mother.

Mom laughed. "This was just the first day," she reminded me, "and it's a holiday weekend. We'll have to see how the rest of the summer goes. But we made twice what I expected we would!"

With a grunt Rose got up from the floor. "If Daisy were here, she'd say you'd hit a home run, Mom. I think this calls for a celebration. Let's eat."

"Let's go out," Mom said with a grin. "I think we've had enough of our own cooking for the day."

Ten

For the next couple of weeks the scene at Potluck wasn't as crazy as it had been over Memorial Day weekend, but business was still lively. The shop was a success by any measure.

I found that I really liked working with Laurel. One day, after taking care of a customer who wanted a pound of tabbouleh and half a dozen lemon squares, Laurel came out from behind the counter and helped me unpack a crate of our old neighbor Sue Smith's homemade jams and jellies. "I like this shop, don't you?" I asked Laurel.

She nodded. "Everything's so appealing. No wonder people can't come in here and buy just one thing. Mrs. Smith's jams are selling really well."

"I think it's great that Mom's selling a lot of local stuff."

"Me too," Laurel agreed.

"So, who gets the first lunch break today?" I asked. She and I had been taking turns.

"I don't mind waiting," she answered.

I got to my feet. "I'll head out, then."

"Where are you going?"

"Probably the bookstore. How about you?"

"I think I'll run up and get Snickers and then take a quick walk in the park," Laurel said. "That's the only thing I don't like about working here—being cooped up inside all day."

"See you later," I said as I headed out the door.

I'd been spending most of my lunch breaks at Harbor Light Books since it was right across the street. Daniel worked there, and he always had some new book to recommend to me, and I'd write down the title so I could look for it at the library. If I found something I just had to own, he'd pretend he was buying it for himself so he could give me his employee discount. Some days I went to visit Seth; he worked down by the beach, at a surf shop. They sold cool sunglasses and stuff, and Seth said that being near the ocean was like "standing beside the muse." But I didn't feel like going to see him today.

I jogged up to the Down East News and Drugstore to buy a candy bar. Back at Harbor Light Books, I paused outside to look at the window display and then sailed in, ready to greet Daniel with a smile. Instead Mr. Ballard, the elderly guy, was behind the cash register. "Hi, Mr. Ballard," I said. "Is Daniel around?"

"He just headed out on his lunch break," Mr. Ballard answered, adjusting his bifocals.

"Oh." My smile faded. "Do you know when he'll be back?"

"He's usually gone for an hour."

We only took half-hour breaks at Potluck. I

won't see him today, I realized, strangely disappointed. Not that it should matter. I could look at books just as well without him. "Thanks, Mr. Ballard," I said. "I'll just browse around." It was odd to realize that I'd been counting on seeing Daniel.

I wandered up and down the aisles for a few minutes, then headed back outside to the sidewalk without buying anything. The bookstore wasn't nearly as much fun without Daniel there to joke around with.

I still had twenty minutes left in my break, but it wasn't really enough time to run to the surf shop. Or maybe it was. But hanging out with Seth isn't all that relaxing, I admitted to myself. He'd want to read me some of the indecipherable poetry he wrote when he wasn't selling Teva sandals and Bollé glasses. Or we'd have to rehash our analysis of the plot of the obscure foreign movie we'd rented the night before. Plus I wasn't wearing black today—I'd thrown on a flowered shirt and pink shorts. *And* I'd forgotten my glasses.

Instead I went back to Potluck to eat my yogurt and then check the display case to see if there were any lemon squares too crumbly to sell to customers.

Daniel called a couple of nights later. "Sorry I missed you at the store the other day," he said.

"It wasn't a big deal," I assured him, in case he could somehow sense that at the time I'd been bummed.

"Are you writing these days?" he asked.

"I'm totally blocked," I said with a gloomy sigh.

"Really?"

"Really. I sit down with paper and pencil, but nothing happens. I've tried some different things—writing first thing in the morning, writing during my lunch hour, writing before bedtime, listening to music, eating a snack while I write, taking my notebook to the park—but nothing works."

"Why don't we get together and do writing exercises like we used to for Mrs. Cobb's class?"

"You and me?"

"Yeah." He hesitated. "Unless you don't want to. Maybe you'd rather do something like that with Seth."

"Seth informed me yesterday that he's not trying out for Mrs. Cobb's class. He's 'grown beyond it.'"

Daniel laughed. "Not me, man."

"OK, sure, let's do it," I said. "How about this weekend?"

We picked a time to meet at his house. To be honest, I couldn't wait. Just because I wanted to get back to writing, of course.

In my bedroom I sat down at the desk with a narrow-ruled legal pad and a new mechanical pencil. I put the lead to the paper, but my hand didn't move. Write a story about anything, I told myself. It doesn't have to be brilliant. You don't have to make people laugh.

Five minutes later I gave up with a sigh. No

story had materialized—not even the first sentence of one. I turned on my laptop, figuring I could at least write in my journal. I never get blocked writing in my journal.

Five minutes later the screen was still blank. I turned off my computer and got up from the desk. The sun had set. Standing at the window, I stared down at Main Street. As I watched, the streetlights came on one by one. My room was still dark, though, and so was my mood.

If I'm a writer, then how come I can't write? I wondered. I didn't like to admit it, but I was counting on Daniel's help.

Eleven

On Saturday, I drove my stepfather's Subaru to Daniel's house—his family lives a couple of miles inland. I parked it in the driveway and ran to the porch so I wouldn't get soaked.

Just as Daniel was opening the door, a bolt of lightning zigzagged across the charcoal sky. A few seconds later we heard the crack and boom of thunder. "Come inside," Daniel advised, "before you get electrocuted."

I'd never been to his house. "This is nice," I said as he walked me down the hall to the den. "Is it old?"

"Nineteen-ten or something like that."

"We used to live in an old house." I stopped to look at a family portrait on the wall. "Is that *you?*"

I pointed to a little kid with buck teeth and a carrot-colored crew cut. Daniel groaned. "Don't remind me, okay? I'm always after my parents to take that down, but they think it's cute."

"Are your folks home?" I asked. "Can I meet them?"

"They went to the hardware store," Daniel answered. "They should be back before you leave."

119

"How about your brother and sister?" From the picture it looked like Daniel was the middle child.

"My big sister's in summer session at Dartmouth," Daniel said, "and my little brother's at sailing camp."

"My sister went to Dartmouth," I said. "Daisy. The one who died."

Daniel nodded. "I think I knew that."

We didn't speak as we walked into the den and sat down on the couch. Suddenly I shivered.

"Are you cold?" Daniel asked. "I could get you a sweatshirt or something."

I shook my head. "That's okay. It was just . . . weather like this always gets me down. Storms and rainy nights can be pretty bad luck."

Daniel's forehead creased. "I'm sorry I reminded you about your sister. That must make you really sad."

"Sometimes," I admitted. Bending over to hide the tears that were gathering in my eyes, I pulled a notebook from my backpack. "Should we start writing?" I asked, taking a deep breath to regain my composure.

Daniel must have sensed that I didn't really want to talk. "Yes, let's write," he said.

We sat at opposite ends of the sofa, sitting sideways facing each other with our feet up on the cushions and our notebooks propped against our knees. "Let's try some warm-up exercises," Daniel suggested. "How about I give you a topic to write a paragraph about and you give me one? Then we can read our paragraphs out loud."

"Okay." Lightning flashed and thunder rumbled, closer together this time. "Why don't you write about learning how to ride a bicycle?"

"And you write about a visit to the orthodontist."

We wrote our paragraphs, then read them to each other. They were pretty good—full of concrete detail, the way Mrs. Cobb liked them. "Let's do another one," I suggested.

"All right." Daniel gave me a mischievous smile. "This time write about your most embarrassing moment."

I laughed. "Are you kidding?"

"Absolutely not."

"You really want to hear about the time I—"

"No, no," he interrupted, "just write it."

"Okay, then *you* write about your first kiss."

Daniel turned a little red, and I thought he was going to confess that he'd never kissed anyone. Instead he said, "You asked for it!"

I giggled as I wrote my paragraph. Daniel was grinning, too. "You read first," he said.

"Okay." I cleared my throat. "'Picture the scene,'" I began. "'The junior high gymnasium. Songs from the *Grease* soundtrack blast through the crowded room. It's the seventh-grade sock hop. I'm wearing a pink poodle skirt and a fuzzy white cardigan buttoned up backward and my very first bra.'"

Daniel laughed pretty hard when I got to the part about Noelle spilling punch all over my sweater while I was jitterbugging with Jamie

Buckingham and Jamie trying to dry me off by pawing my chest with a paper towel. "Let's hear yours," I said when I was through.

Daniel smiled wryly. "Actually, now that I think about it, my first kiss could also qualify as my most embarrassing moment."

"Doesn't everyone's?" I said reassuringly.

He cleared his throat. "Okay. Here goes."

Daniel's first kiss was at the beginning of ninth grade with Martha Cabot. "Martha Cabot?" I exclaimed. Martha's kind of pretty, but she's about six feet tall. "How did you reach her lips?"

"This is hard enough as it is," Daniel said. "Don't interrupt me."

Covering my mouth with my hand so I wouldn't laugh, I let him finish. He and Martha had been working on the school yearbook together, and one day in the darkroom she'd put the moves on him. Daniel had been so surprised, he'd knocked over a basin of developer.

"That's terrible," I sympathized. I couldn't bump his shoulder because of the way we were sitting, so I nudged his bare foot with mine. "You know what, though? I don't think it should count. Your first kiss should be one you were psyched about. Write another paragraph."

"You write about yours, then," Daniel said.

Instead of writing, I clasped my notebook to my chest. "I was in eighth grade," I recalled. "I kissed Sam Lovejoy at Alyssa Chamberlain's Halloween party."

Daniel hugged his notebook, too. "Okay, so I guess my first *real* kiss was with Debbie DeBernardo. I took her to the Christmas dance when we were freshmen."

Debbie had moved away sophomore year—Ohio or someplace like that. "Did you guys date? Did you like her?"

"She was nice," Daniel said. "We weren't a couple, though."

"Have you ever been a couple with anyone?" I asked.

Daniel blushed a little. "I guess not."

I nudged his foot again. "That's okay. Being a couple isn't always all it's cracked up to be."

"I figure it'll happen when it happens." Daniel looked at me. I'd never really noticed how blue his eyes were. "When the right person comes along."

"That's absolutely the right attitude," I said, trying to sound like I didn't have any doubts.

But Daniel never misses a trick. "Is that how it is with you and Seth?" He was still looking at me intently. "He's the right person?"

"I don't know. I guess so." For some reason I didn't want to talk about Seth. "Back to Debbie D. Was she your dream girl?"

"Not really. She wasn't imaginative enough. What about Jamie Buckingham? Are you still heartbroken that things didn't work out with him?"

I giggled. "Yeah, right. He had the worst taste in clothes! His socks always clashed with his pants."

"What a crime," Daniel kidded.

"Well, it matters to me," I said. "I can't help it."

"Do *I* pass the fashion test?" he asked.

I checked out his faded navy polo shirt and rumpled khakis. "You're conservative, but yes. You match."

"Good."

"Okay, I have another one for you," I said. My knees were getting stiff from being bent, so I stretched my right leg out along the edge of the sofa. My foot was next to Daniel's hip but not touching him. "I've heard about your first kiss. What was your *best* kiss?"

Daniel lifted his eyes to the ceiling. "What's happening here? We're not even writing. It's like truth or dare or something."

"It's fun," I said. "Isn't it?"

"Kind of." He thought for a while, then smiled crookedly. He'd put his notebook down, and now he folded his arms across his chest. He has a decent body, I found myself noticing. Not as skinny as I thought. "I don't think I've had my best kiss yet," he said. "I'm still waiting for it. What about you?"

"Has to be my first kiss with Seth," I said, but suddenly I wasn't so sure. *Was* that my best kiss? Or was I still waiting, too?

While we'd been talking, lightning and thunder had continued to flicker and rumble while rain lashed the windowpanes. Daniel's house seemed to be right in the middle of the storm. Now, all at once, there was a brilliant flash at the window, accompanied by a resounding boom. Instantly the lights went out.

I let out a startled squeak.

"There goes the power," Daniel observed.

"I hope it doesn't start a fire or anything."

"Don't worry. Our power's always going out. There are too many trees around here with branches leaning on the lines. Should I light a candle?"

"If you want."

He didn't move, though. We stared at each other in the dim light. We were still sitting on the couch, and now he put a hand on my bare ankle, the one that was closest to him. I nudged his toes with my other foot. The room seemed full of electricity; a serious shiver ran up my spine. "Lily," Daniel said softly.

"Don't say anything," I whispered.

I'm not sure what possessed me. Maybe it was all that talk about the perfect kiss and the sudden convenient darkness. Maybe it was just something I'd subconsciously wanted to do for a long time. Anyway, I shifted on the couch, getting on my knees so I could reach over and rest my hands on Daniel's shoulders. Then I kissed him.

If he was surprised, he didn't act it. He grasped my waist in his hands and kissed me right back. With the storm rumbling around us, we kept on kissing. And it was a *great* kiss. Possibly the best kiss ever.

*   *   *

"Laurel, I need to make a confession," I told my sister that night.

"What do I look like, a priest?" she joked.

The two of us had gone out for pizza because Mom and Hal were at a dinner party. Now I looked over my shoulder to double check that there was nobody I knew in Pizza Bowl to overhear this. "I kissed a guy," I said, lowering my voice. "A guy who wasn't Seth."

Laurel raised her eyebrows. "Interesting."

"Interesting? It's awful. It's cheating! I cheated on my boyfriend." I clapped a hand over my mouth. "Oh no! What if someone heard me say that?"

"No one heard," Laurel assured me. "Just tell me what happened."

I gave her a brief sketch of my afternoon at Daniel's, including the abrupt ending: His parents had gotten home from the hardware store and, despite the storm, I'd taken off like I'd been shot from a cannon. "I don't know what came over me," I concluded. "There must have been some weird charge in the air from the storm."

"Maybe you like him," Laurel said, reaching for another slice of pizza.

"Sure, I like him, but I don't *like* him."

"Why not?" She'd met him a couple of times. "He seems like a neat guy to me."

"Well, first of all, he's not as good-looking as Seth," I told Laurel. "I mean, Daniel's just average."

"So?" she said. "Looks don't mean everything."

"You can afford to say that because Carlos is a total stud."

Laurel shrugged. "He's cute, but that's incidental. I fell for him because we bonded over stuff. We care about the same things. We look at the world in the same way."

I thought about it. What kinds of things did Seth and I bond over? What did he care about? His clothes, his reputation . . . "Wait a minute," I said, confused. "Let's get back to the cheating thing. I'm going out with Seth. I shouldn't be kissing another guy no matter *who* he is."

"That's true," Laurel agreed, "but you can't go back in time and undo it, so you might as well try to understand why it happened. Why *did* it?"

I thought back. "Well, we were just having this really fun time writing and talking, and after a while it got personal. And our feet were touching." I told Laurel about how we were sitting on the couch. "Then I started to get this tingly feeling, like I was more aware of him physically. And it's not that Daniel and I see things in the exact same way, like you and Carlos. We disagree a lot. But we have fun arguing."

"Well, let's talk about Seth," Laurel suggested. "Do you and he have fun talking?"

"Yeah, sure," I said.

"What do you talk about?"

"You name it. We're *always* talking about intellectual things. And we talk about other people. We're sarcastic together."

"Is that enough?" Laurel asked.

I stared at her. "What do you mean?"

"I mean, does it make you happy? Maybe you kissed Daniel because there's something missing in your relationship with Seth."

I wrinkled my forehead. "How could there be? Seth's gorgeous and cool, and Daniel's not."

Laurel shrugged again. "You're the one who kissed Daniel, not me."

We finished our pizza in silence.

Walking to the car in the parking lot, I asked Laurel, "So what do I do now?"

"You mean about the guys?"

"Yeah."

"I guess you either stay with Seth because you like him best and write the other thing off as a fluke, or you break up with Seth and possibly explore something new with Daniel."

"Well, which?"

Laurel laughed. "*You* have to decide, Lil. I can't figure out your feelings for you. Believe me, it's hard enough most of the time figuring out my own."

We drove home, listening to the radio. Laurel was behind the wheel, so I stared out the window at the dark night woods and tried to decode my feelings. It was trickier than you might think. On the surface, it seemed like a no-brainer. I was dating Seth Modine, and in the world of Hawk Harbor, that was about as good as it gets. But if that was true, then why had I kissed Daniel . . . and why did I think that if I had the chance, I'd do it again?

*   *   *

"I'm completely confused about my love life," I typed in my journal early Tuesday evening. *"I'm avoiding Seth and Daniel—I just can't deal with either of them right now. Seth wanted to come over tonight, but I lied and told him I have a fever. Daniel must've been as flipped out as I was about our kiss on Saturday during the thunderstorm. He hasn't called to talk about writing or anything else. And I'm not sure how I feel about that. Maybe I'll try writing a story so that if he calls, we'll have something to talk about besides us."*

I put away my computer and got out a pad of paper and a mechanical pencil. Moving my desk chair over by my bed, I sat with my feet propped on the mattress and my face turned to the view through the window of the harbor in the last light of a clear summer day. "What should I write about?" I asked a sailboat with a deep green hull. My heart was so full—I wanted just to pour it out onto the page. I clicked my pencil and began scribbling, but when I saw the first two words I'd written, I stopped. *"Dear Daisy . . ."*

I tossed my notebook and pencil on the bed and hugged my knees to my chin, rocking myself and crying. "I miss you so much right now, Daze," I whispered. "I've never felt this alone before."

I looked out the window again, my eyes blurry with tears. The green sailboat was at its mooring now, and its sails were being reefed for the night. I didn't feel Daisy's presence—I felt alone, more alone than I'd ever felt in my entire life.

Twelve

I was drying my hands on a dish towel when the phone rang. Laurel and I had just cleaned up from dinner. I picked up the receiver. "Hello?"

"Lily? It's Daniel."

"Hi, Daniel," I said. I shot a glance at Laurel. "What's up?"

"I thought maybe we could get together. Just to talk."

"You mean tonight? Right now?"

"Yeah, if you're free. I'll buy you an ice-cream cone," he offered.

"Okay," I agreed. "Meet you at the Corner Ice Cream Shoppe in half an hour."

I hung up the phone. "You made a date with Daniel?" Laurel guessed.

"Ice cream doesn't count as a date," I said. "But we *are* going to 'talk.'"

"What are you going to say to him?" my sister asked.

I heaved a troubled sigh. "I have no idea."

I was on the way out the door to meet Daniel when the phone rang again. This time when I picked it up, I heard another very familiar male voice. "Lily, I haven't seen you in days," Seth said.

"It's been kind of busy here."

"Let's go out and you can tell me about it."

I hesitated. Since I didn't know what I was going to say to Daniel, I didn't know how long our nondate would take. But I probably needed to "talk" to Seth, too. "Why don't we meet in an hour?" I suggested. "By the surf shop—we can take a walk on the beach."

"See you there."

As I walked down the street to the ice-cream place, I struggled to understand my emotions. They were all over the map. What do you want, Lily Rebecca Walker? I asked myself. Did I want to stay with Seth? I liked being his girlfriend well enough, but was well enough *enough?* Now that a few months had passed, the initial thrill had worn off a little. I still found him incredibly attractive, but I had to be honest with myself. His friends were starting to get on my nerves. They were cool, but they never had any fun. Seth was smart, but even so, our relationship didn't have a whole lot of depth.

Still, everybody at South Regional will think I'm crazy if I break up with Seth to go out with Daniel, I thought. It will blow my whole image. My image. That phrase stopped me. I'd been cultivating this image the whole year since I'd turned sixteen. The black clothes, the too-cool-to-care cynicism, the anything-for-a-laugh poems and stories. Now I touched the rectangular glasses perching on my nose. I was tired of them and everything they symbolized.

Maybe it's time to ditch the image, I thought. Maybe other people's opinions have nothing to do with this. Maybe I need to do what's right for me.

Outside the Corner Ice Cream Shoppe, I paused. I saw Daniel inside, sitting at one of the little wrought iron tables. He didn't see me, though—he was looking up at the list of flavors posted on the wall—so I had an extra minute to think. For a few seconds I was overcome with longing. I wanted to muss Daniel's rumpled auburn hair with my fingers and have him say sweetly comforting, encouraging words. Daniel, who'd liked me, I realized now, since the winter day we became writing partners.

But even while half of me wanted to fling myself in Daniel's arms, the other half panicked. I got a nervous, sick feeling in my stomach. I can't do it, I thought. I couldn't break up with Seth and start fresh with Daniel or anybody. Things had been going so well for me—was I really ready to throw it all away?

I pushed open the door and a bell jingled. Daniel turned around. "Hi, Lily," he said, his cheeks getting kind of pink.

"Daniel, I'm not really hungry for ice cream," I said. "Can we just take a walk instead?"

"Sure."

We headed outside and turned down a quiet side street. I started talking before Daniel could say anything that would end up making us both feel worse than we were bound to feel, anyway. "Daniel, after this . . . I can't see you again."

There was a pause. "Oh," he said finally.

I looked at him. He was staring straight ahead, his jaw clenched. "I'm sorry," I went on quickly. "I know the other day it must have seemed like I . . . had feelings for you. But I don't. Kissing you was a mistake. I'm still Seth's girlfriend."

"I see."

"You do?"

"Yeah, it's pretty clear," Daniel said simply. "I made a mistake, too. I thought you could see beyond the superficial stuff. But I was wrong. Sorry I'm not cool enough for you, Lily."

His voice was full of pain, and my heart ached. I hated hurting him, especially because I knew that *he* would never hurt *me* like this.

He'd turned sharply around to walk back to town. "Daniel, wait," I called after him. I couldn't take back my words, but I wanted to make things better somehow. "It's not like that. I swear."

He didn't wait, though. And I wasn't so sure that it wasn't "like that."

I stood on the sidewalk, watching him go. My eyes were dry; it's possible, I'd learned lately, to be too sad to cry.

I checked my watch. I still had some time to kill before my beach date with Seth. My talk with

Daniel—our last, I guessed—had taken a lot less than an hour.

The next day during my lunch break I rode my bike to Mrs. Cobb's house. I was hoping she wouldn't be home, so I could just stick the envelope in her mailbox, but when I rang the bell, she came to the door. "Lily, hi," she said with a warm smile. "Are you submitting a manuscript for the writing class?"

I nodded. "I didn't write much all summer, but last night for some reason I got motivated." After finishing my journal entry, I'd stayed up until midnight writing a tragicomic story about a teenage girl who gets amnesia after a bizarre electrolysis accident.

"Well, you're just in time," Mrs. Cobb told me. "I'm almost done reading the submissions. I'll be able to let you know in a couple of days whether you'll have a spot in the class."

"Not much chance, huh?" I asked glumly.

"There's a perfectly good chance."

"But you don't even really like my writing."

"That's not true," Mrs. Cobb said. "I think you have a vibrant, colorful imagination and a rich vocabulary." She gave my envelope a shake. "I'll look forward to reading what's in here."

"Well . . . thanks." I kicked at a loose brick on the walkway. "Did, um, Daniel Levin try out for the class?"

"Yes, along with about thirty others, including you."

"Thirty?" I gulped. "For a class of fifteen?"

She nodded.

I said good-bye to Mrs. Cobb and rode my bike back to town. With that much competition I didn't have a prayer of getting into the writing class. It was hard not to care, even though I tried.

Toward the end of summer Laurel and Mom started having whispery conversations that they'd cut short the moment I entered the room. I had no idea what was brewing until the weekend Carlos came up from Tufts for a visit.

Carlos was cheerful with the rest of us, but I couldn't help picking up on some extremely tense vibes between him and Laurel. After lunch one Sunday, Mom went up to her room for a rest, and Laurel and Carlos ducked into the family room. They didn't close the door all the way, so naturally I took this as an open invitation to eavesdrop.

"I can't believe you're dropping out," Carlos said to Laurel.

My eyes widened. Dropping out?

"I'm not dropping out," Laurel countered. "I'm taking time off. That's a completely different thing."

"How is it different?" Carlos asked. "It sounds the same to me."

"I'll go back for spring semester," she told him, "or next fall at the latest. I won't lose that much time. I just need to get my head together. And my mom needs me—the store is only starting to get off the ground."

"Of course you want to help your mom," Carlos said, his tone softening. "But I'm worried that you're using the store as an excuse because you were bummed about your grades last year. I'm worried that taking time off will make it easier not to go back at all."

Laurel was quiet for a minute. I held my breath, waiting for her response. "I don't think I'm looking for an excuse," she said at last. "I don't feel like I'm wimping out. I just feel like I don't know what I want right now. Can you accept that?"

Carlos must have given her the kind of answer that doesn't require words because the room fell silent. I tiptoed away. That's the big secret, then, I thought. Laurel's taking time off from college to help Mom. It was hard for me to see that as a problem. As far as I was concerned, it would be great to have my sister around a while longer. What about me, though? Why did Mom need Laurel's help so badly? Wasn't *I* good for anything?

Thirteen

The next night Laurel and I talked about my new work schedule. She was practically running Potluck now, with Hal's help—he'd cut back his accounting practice so he could be more involved with Mom's businesses. Mom was focused on the catering end.

Since school was about to start, Laurel had me down for just the Saturday shift. "I could do more, you know," I told her.

"Let's see how it goes," she replied. "With college interviews and applications and the creative-writing workshop on top of everything else, you'll be pretty busy."

I'd gotten into Mrs. Cobb's writing class—that had been a pretty nice surprise. Mickey had gotten in, too, and I was glad I'd have an excuse to see her more. Other than that, for the first time in my life I wasn't that psyched about a new school year.

Seth picked me up on Monday morning. As we drove along, Seth cranked the volume on the jazz station. I stared out the window.

The lobby of South Regional was packed with excited bodies. Everybody was talking a mile a

minute, laughing, shouting. Seth waded into the
mob with all the confidence of a senior.

I trailed after him as he greeted his friends and
bumped right into him when he stopped abruptly.
"Who's that?" he asked, staring.

I followed his gaze. A girl I'd never seen before was standing at the foot of the big staircase.
She was pencil thin with very short, black hair,
pale skin, and huge doe eyes. Her mouth was a
dramatic slash of dark lipstick. "I don't know," I
said.

Rico loomed up behind us. "Simona van der
Wilde," he reported into Seth's ear. "Sophomore.
Just moved here."

"Simona van der Wilde?" I couldn't help giggling.

"Hmmm," Seth murmured.

I didn't pay much attention to Simona van der
Wilde. Maybe I should have. Four days later, after
school on Friday, Seth took me for a drive.

And dumped me.

"I'm really sorry, Lily," he said. We were
parked near the lighthouse. "I don't know how it
happened. There's just this intense spiritual and
intellectual connection between me and Simona.
And you and me . . . it's not there anymore. I want
to get to know her better, and I'm not about to go
behind your back."

"Oh," I said, stunned. Seth was watching me,
and I felt like I should show some emotion—start
screaming or crying or hitting him or something.
But I didn't feel anything except an absurd desire

to laugh. Spiritual and intellectual connection? I'm sure! "Wow."

"If you ever need a friend, I'll still be there for you, okay?" Seth traced my cheekbone with a gentle finger.

"Okay."

Seth hugged me. "I knew you'd be objective about this. Thanks."

We headed back to town. Seth stopped in front of my building. Before I got out of the car, he leaned over and kissed me on the cheek. "Take care of yourself, Lily."

"I will."

I stepped out onto the curb. Then after Seth drove off, I experienced a major delayed reaction. It's over, I thought, tears springing to my eyes. We broke up. And because of someone named Simona van der Wilde!

As I walked up to the apartment, though, I knew it wasn't totally Simona's fault. Seth was right—he and I hadn't been clicking for a while. At least he'd been honest about wanting to date someone new.

I dumped my book bag on the floor in the front hall and shuffled into the kitchen. There was a plate of Potluck brownies on the counter—I helped myself to one, along with a glass of milk. I was sitting at the table with my snack, trying to take Seth's picture out of my locket, when Mom came in, wearing a bathrobe. "What's up?" she asked.

I dug at the little photo with my fingernail, and it finally popped out. "Gotcha," I declared.

Mom sat down next to me and watched me tear the tiny picture to shreds. "Did you and Seth have a fight?"

I told her about Simona. "It's not like it was a match made in heaven," I said, sniffling. "But we were a *couple*. I could depend on that. Now I'm on my own again."

Mom patted my shoulder. "I know what it's like. Even when you've outgrown a relationship, it always hurts to say good-bye to someone you've cared about."

"I hadn't necessarily *outgrown* the relationship," I said.

"No?"

We sat in silence for a minute. I kept sniffling and Mom kept rubbing my shoulder. "Well, maybe I had, a little," I conceded. "It wasn't working, anyway."

"You know what I think?" Mom said. "Remember when you were younger, you were always going through phases? Well, I think Lily Walker is about to enter a new phase."

I looked at her with my arms folded. "A new phase. Great," I groaned.

Mom laughed. "What's wrong with that? Why should you have to stick to just one?"

"Because I felt like I'd finally settled down," I said. "People knew who I was. It's like how it was for Daisy."

"Daisy?" Mom said, puzzled.

"Daisy had her act together," I explained. "She was in control of her destiny. She knew what she was good at, and she knew what she wanted to accomplish, and people liked and admired her for it. Nothing bothered her," I added. "She was so strong."

Mom shook her head. "No one loved Daisy more than I did, but she was *not* perfect."

"I didn't say she was *perfect*," I said. "Well . . . maybe."

"Daisy went through phases, too," Mom reminded me. "Remember when *she* was sixteen? She tore those ligaments in her knee and had to sit out soccer *and* basketball seasons. She had a hard time finding the right way to mourn your father. And I—all of us—were putting too much pressure on her always to be strong, cheerful Daisy."

"She kind of went wild," I recalled. It was true. But she'd gotten over it and come out stronger.

"She went through a phase," Mom said. "And do you know what?"

"What?"

"If she were alive today, chances are she'd be going through some other phase."

"I don't think so." I pictured the photograph on my desk. "Not Daisy."

"Yes," Mom insisted. "It could have been anything. She might have decided she was tired of sports. Maybe she would have spent her junior

year abroad or taken time off from college alto-
gether for some reason, like Laurel. She might
have changed her mind about being premed and
decided to be a teacher or a banker or an . . . an as-
trologer instead."

I laughed.

"My point is, Lil, we *all* evolve. It never stops.
Daisy might seem unchanging and somehow larger
than life because you remember her as she was at
nineteen, and that's all we'll ever know for sure.
She didn't get to live out her life. But if she had, I
guarantee there would have been some surprises
in it."

I looked at my mother. There were lines etched
around her large blue eyes—lines she had earned
caring for me and my sisters, and starting a business, and learning to be independent—but they
were warm and beautiful eyes.

Suddenly I knew whose picture I wanted to put
in my locket. I wanted a picture of Mom, as she
was right at this moment. She held out her arms to
hug me, and I rested my head on her shoulder.
"Thanks, Mom," I whispered.

It was unbelievable how fast the It crowd
dropped me after I stopped dating Seth. "Easy
come, easy go," I said to Mickey and Noelle one
day at lunch in the school cafeteria.

"Who needs them?" Noelle declared loyally. I
couldn't believe how nice they were being. After
all, I hadn't treated them that well last spring. But

as Noelle had said the night I called to tell her that Seth and I broke up, "Good friends know how to forgive and forget."

I cast a glance at a table halfway across the cafeteria. I was trying not to get bummed out about the spectacle of my ex sharing a chair and a cappuccino with Simona van der Wilde.

Unwrapping my tuna salad sandwich, I said in my noblest tone, "I don't really hold a grudge. I hope they'll be very happy together."

Mickey and Noelle stared at me for a second, then burst out laughing. I had to laugh, too. "Yeah, right!" they said.

We finished our sandwiches, treating ourselves to candy bars from the vending machine on our way out of the cafeteria. "You know, there is at least one good thing about you and Seth breaking up," Mickey commented as we walked down the hall toward our lockers.

"What?" I asked.

"You're wearing fun clothes again instead of all that basic black."

I looked down at my outfit: rainbow-striped tights and a red jumper. At breakfast that morning Laurel had told me I looked a little like Ronald McDonald. Best of all, I'd tossed out those glasses.

The previous winter and spring I'd created a new persona for myself: I was the girl who entertained people with her sarcasm and who dressed like a chic but colorless waif. By summertime I hadn't really wanted to be that Lily Walker anymore, but I was stuck with her because she was the one who was dating Seth Modine. Now I was free again to be whoever I wanted to be.

Which brought me back to the same old dilemma. Who am I? What kind of stories do I want to write?

That night at home I tried to work on my creative-writing assignment. The topic was to write a story based on an epigram, like "forgive and forget" or "make hay while the sun shines," but as usual lately I was totally blocked. *"Make hay, make hay,"* I scribbled over and over in my notebook. *"Forgive and forget, forgive and forget, forgive and forget."*

I wanted to call up Daniel like in the old days, but we weren't really speaking much even though he had to know I wasn't seeing Seth any longer. He was taking Mrs. Cobb's class, too, and he was polite to me, but that was about it.

I thought about writing the kind of story I'd churned out for class all last spring, but I couldn't bring myself to do it. That had never been my real voice, whatever my real voice was. And Mrs. Cobb had told me she let me into the class because I had potential and she wanted me to discover it. I owed it to her to try.

I sat on my bed for a minute, gazing pensively into space. My window was open, and a mild September breeze stirred the curtain. Suddenly I found myself remembering the day Mom, Rose, and I had climbed up to the attic to look for old baby clothes. Mom had found my great-grandmother's diaries. What had she said? "Maybe they'll give you some ideas for stories...."

Hopping off the bed, I walked over to my closet. I'd stuck the cardboard box under a pile of old sweaters. Now I moved the sweaters aside and reached into the box, pulling out a small, leather-bound volume.

I opened it up. Flora Elizabeth White had written her name, the place, and the date on the inside cover in a cursive as flowery as her name. People really shouldn't read other people's diaries, even if they *have* been dead twenty years, I thought, but I turned to the first entry, anyway.

"*My dear Diary and Friend,*" Flora wrote. "*Today is my sixteenth birthday. Sixteen! Doesn't that sound old? We're celebrating with ice cream—my little brother Billy will have to turn the handle all by himself—and a picnic by the sea. I'll wear my new bathing dress, which shows quite a bit of leg ... sure to scandalize this buttoned-up town! Do you suppose that now that I'm a grown woman, Mama and Papa will allow me to receive suitors as they did Eleanor when she turned sixteen? I know Simon Walker is dying to pay me a call!*"

Four pages later Flora's tone grew more serious. "*It is as we feared, Diary. As you know, my sister Eleanor's health hasn't been good for some time. Last week the doctor made the dreaded diagnosis: galloping consumption—tuberculosis. Since then Eleanor seems to fade more each day. I worry that she's giving up hope.*

We must *believe she'll be cured! How could I go on if she were taken from me?"*

I almost couldn't believe what I was reading. It seemed so immediate, so present. It's exactly like what I went through losing Daisy, I thought. I turned the page quickly. I had to find out. What would happen to Eleanor? Would she be all right?

There was an entry dated a month later. *"Mother and Eleanor left yesterday on the train, heading west to Arizona, where they'll stay two months. It's hard to be separated from my only sister, but maybe it's for the best. I need to learn to be less reliant on her and more reliant on myself. But it's difficult, Diary. She's not just my sister; she's my dearest friend."*

I found myself nodding as I read. Yes, I thought. I know exactly what you mean.

Flora continued, describing the reason for the trip. *"The doctor says a dry climate is the best thing for Eleanor's condition and that the damp summer air in Hawk Harbor is terribly unhealthy. I took a walk by the sea this afternoon, waiting for Papa to return on his fishing boat, and it's very hard for me to believe that the salty breeze is anything but wholesome. But Dr. Lovejoy must know best, mustn't he?"*

On the next page Flora's mood lightened up. *"Simon Walker paid a call this evening. Didn't I tell you he would? He didn't enjoy himself as much as he might have, however, because Harding Quayle got here first. You should have seen me, Diary! Calmly mending Papa's fishing nets on the porch swing while Harding and Simon argued about politics. Two suitors in one evening! Harding is a better conversationalist, but I suspect that sometimes he speaks just to hear the sound of his own voice."*

"Sounds familiar," I said aloud.

"Whereas Simon seems more thoughtful," Flora wrote. *"And I know I'm not supposed to judge a book by its cover, but Simon also happens to be the handsomest boy in Hawk Harbor."*

I couldn't stop reading. When I finished one volume, I dove immediately into the next. Flora's diary was better than a novel. There were so many ups and downs. Eleanor returned from Arizona, her health improved, only to die of scarlet fever a year later. The pages where Flora wrote about that were tear-stained and, reading about it, I cried, too. *"It's as if my heart has been torn from my body,"* Flora mourned. I knew exactly how she'd felt.

I kept reading. Flora's family survived hard times and easy ones. Simon kept on courting Flora even though there were always other guys hanging around, and he even got up his nerve to propose to her, but she turned him down.

"Why did you do that?" I exclaimed. "You *have* to marry him, Flora. He's my great-grandfather!"

Sure enough, after Simon went off and proposed to another girl (Dorothea Lovejoy, the doctor's daughter), Flora came to her senses and told him she *did* love him in a scene that poor Dorothea happened to witness, so needless to say, she broke up with Simon, who then reproposed to Flora, who finally said yes.

Flora's diaries covered it all: baptisms and funerals, blizzards and croquet games, tea parties and presidential elections. She liked clothes as much as I did and described what she wore on every occasion. I felt like I'd made a new friend.

It got a little less interesting after she had babies, though. Closing the diary, I put it on my shelf with the other volumes. "I'll finish reading this a few years down the road," I promised my great-grandmother, "when I can relate to it a little more. In the meantime maybe Rose would get into it!"

I sat at my window, looking out at Hawk Harbor in the moonlight. Flora's diaries had put a lot of things in new perspective, like my breakup with Seth. It was weird, thinking that the young woman who'd kept that journal had grown up and grown old and finally died. Weird, but natural. She coped, I thought. Life brought her bad as well as good, but more good than bad. She flourished even without her big sister around to take care of her. She had a long, interesting life.

A feeling of peace entered me. I decided I didn't want to write anything of my own just then—I wanted to absorb what I'd read.

What I'd learned.

Fourteen

"Those diaries sound cool. I *would* like to read them," Rose said.

It was early October, and Rose had come up for the weekend because some of her old Hawk Harbor friends had thrown her a baby shower on Saturday. After the party she, Laurel, and I were sitting on a park bench, enjoying the afternoon sunshine.

Rose placed a hand on her round belly. "Did Flora write anything about what it feels like to have a baby? You know, labor and delivery?"

I shook my head. "No details. She didn't even write that she was *pregnant*. All of a sudden the first baby just *appeared*."

"I guess people didn't talk about that stuff as much as we do nowadays," Rose mused.

"How does it feel?" Laurel asked, kind of shyly. "I mean, this part. *Before* the labor and delivery."

"Well, it feels like—," Rose began. Then she grabbed Laurel's hand and placed it on top of her sweatshirt where it was stretched over her stomach. "See for yourself."

They sat like that for a few seconds. Then Laurel's eyes widened. "Is that the *baby?*"

Rose laughed. "Yep."

"What's it doing?" I asked.

"Back flips!" Laurel said.

I took a turn. I felt something shaped like an elbow sticking up from Rose's abdomen. It swam from one side to the other. "It's like a horror movie," I said. "*Alien.*"

"Gee, thanks," Rose said dryly.

"Isn't it incredible?" Laurel still looked amazed. "There's a *person* in there. A new person."

"I know." Rose nodded, suddenly solemn. "He or she is going to be the start of the next generation of our family."

We all thought about that for a while. "Wow," I said.

"Don't think I'm crazy," Rose went on, "but sometimes I get this eerie feeling. Like I'm a link between the past and the future. Some part of everybody is in me: Mom and Dad, my grandparents, my *great*-grandparents. And it's all going into this baby. He—she—*is* the future, but the past is in her, too."

"That's not only crazy, it's depressing," Laurel said.

Rose shifted position on the bench, then brushed a strand of blond hair off her forehead. "Why?"

"Don't you sometimes want to forget the past?" Laurel asked. "Or parts of it, anyway? It's not like we have the happiest family history."

"That's true," Rose admitted. "But you know what I think? We wouldn't be who we are without our past, even the painful parts. Even the mistakes we've made and the losses we've experienced. It's all part of who we are."

"I wish Daisy were here," I said softly.

Rose took my hand and pressed it. "Me too." Then she laughed. "How did this conversation get so cosmic?"

"If Daisy were here, she wouldn't let us just veg out like this," Laurel speculated. "She'd have you on your feet doing prenatal aerobics."

We all laughed. "Can you imagine?" Rose said, slumping more comfortably on the bench.

"Back to the past stuff," I said. "If Daisy were here—"

"But she *is* here," Rose interrupted. "She's always with us, in a way."

"What way?" I asked.

"Oh, I don't know." Rose thought. "Like when I'm sad about something or scared. I think about Daisy, and not because she had all the answers or anything like that. Not because she was brave, even though she was. I think about her because she loved me and I loved her. It's that simple. I think about *all* the people I love, especially you guys. That's what gets me through."

I looked at my sister, my eyes bright with tears. I wanted to tell Rose how much her words meant to me, but I couldn't speak. "It's all right, Lily," she said softly as she took my hand again. "You can remember Daisy any way you want. Just keep her with you."

I nodded.

Laurel was sniffling. "Can we be a little less heart wrenching?" she asked. "Before we all start bawling in the middle of the park?"

Rose smiled. "Okay, here's some news that will cheer you up. Guess what I've been working on?"

"What?" I asked.

"I cut a demo," she said. "An album!"

Laurel and I both shrieked. "An *album?*"

Rose nodded. "I wasn't going to tell you unless something came of it, but you might as well know so you can be rooting for me. This friend of mine who works at a recording studio got me some time there, and I recorded a bunch of songs. Stuff I wrote and covers. Just me with this guitarist—very bare bones. But people who've heard the tape really like it, so my agent's taking it around to a bunch of music industry people to see if anyone will give me a contract."

Laurel and I shrieked again.

Rose laughed. "Nothing's happened yet. Believe me, you'll be the first to know."

I patted Rose's stomach. "You should be very proud of your mommy, little Jane or David," I declared.

"It's not little Jane or David anymore," Rose said. "Stephen and I realized we weren't wild about those names."

"Who's it going to be, then?" Laurel asked.

"We still haven't decided." Rose's eyes grew dreamy. "All we know is that we want our perfect baby to have a perfect name."

"You've still got some time," I said. "You're not due for seven or eight weeks."

"Right," Rose agreed. "Plenty of time."

The next day after church Rose drove home to Boston. While Hal worked on the computer, Laurel did some reading, and Mom took a nap, I rode my bike to the cemetery with three small pots of gold and russet mums in the handlebar basket.

It had been a long time since I'd visited Dad and Daisy's graves. I just got so busy when I was dating Seth and so into the whole It scene, and sitting in a cemetery talking to your dead sister would *not* have seemed cool to those people. Why did I ever care what they thought? I wondered now.

The graveyard was peaceful. Fallen leaves and cloud shadows danced among the headstones. I placed a flowerpot on Daisy's grave and another one on Dad's. "We miss you guys a lot," I said after a moment. "You watch over us, though, don't you?"

The only answer was the sound of a gray squirrel chattering on a fence rail. "I need to believe that you're still with me, Daze," I said, "the way Rose and Laurel and I were talking yesterday." A tear rolled down my face and dropped silently onto my sister's grave.

I sat right down on the short, golden grass and buried my face in my hands and cried. I cried about breaking up with Seth and losing Daniel's friendship, about Daisy, and about Dad. "I'll never grow up, will I?" I asked. "I'll always be the baby of the family."

That's when I felt it. It's not like I had a visitation or anything like that. I don't believe in ghosts. But all of a sudden I felt this presence. This love.

My sister's love.

Suddenly everything finally made sense because, paradoxically, I finally accepted that it never *would* make sense. That's life. It's not all wrapped up with a tidy bow—it's crazy and disorganized and unpredictable, and so are the people who live it. Growing up doesn't happen overnight—it takes years, decades, a whole lifetime.

I sat for a few more minutes, savoring this feeling. Then I got to my feet, touching Daisy's headstone lightly with my fingertips as I did so. "Thanks," I whispered.

Back at my bike, I remembered the third pot of mums. I picked it up and wandered back into the graveyard, looking for something in particular. Looking for some*one*.

I found her in the far northwest corner of the cemetery, her simple granite headstone in the shade of a red maple. Flora White Walker, it read. And there was Simon's stone, too, right next to hers.

I placed the flowers halfway between the two

graves. "I feel like I know you," I told them softly, "even though we never met. You're part of me, like Rose was saying yesterday. I'm glad."

I pedaled back toward town. Instead of going straight home, though, I found myself cruising down Lighthouse Road.

When I got to my old driveway, I stopped. The Lilac Inn was still for sale. The grass in the front yard was overgrown, and the driveway was carpeted with leaves. I used to live here, I thought as I pushed my bike up the driveway and then propped it against the barn, so it's not *really* trespassing.

I never go anywhere without paper and pencil—there was a notepad in the bike's basket with a mechanical pencil stuck through the spiral wire. Sliding it into my back jeans pocket, I walked across the lawn to a grove of gnarled, ancient apple trees.

I plucked an apple from a low branch and dropped to the grass, sitting with my back against the tree's scratchy trunk. I rubbed the apple clean on my shirt and took a bite.

As I crunched the apple I gazed around the yard that used to be my playground when I was a child. It had been so long since we'd moved—almost eight years—but something about this autumn day, with its misty, earthy smells and ripe colors, made my memories feel vivid and fresh. Something about the conversations I'd had recently with my sisters and my mother, and reading Flora's journals, made the past feel very much alive.

Half closing my eyes, I pictured my younger self, dressed in various silly costumes—cowgirl, pirate, princess—and playing tricks on my big sisters. I remembered one fall day Daisy had spent hours raking up the leaves. I'd ticked off Rose by hanging her underwear and bras on the front porch railing when I knew one of her boyfriends was coming over, so she'd chased me around the yard, and we scattered the leaves all over the place. Laurel kept a bunch of wild animals in hutches by the barn, and I used to feed them Froot Loops because I knew that would make her mad. "We'd go to McCloskey's Farm to pick a pumpkin for Halloween," I reminisced out loud. "Dad helped me carve the best jack-o'-lanterns—one year we made a salty old fisherman with Dad's cap and a Popeye wink and a pipe in the corner of its mouth."

Right about then I got a really peculiar feeling. It was kind of like the one I'd felt at the cemetery—the presence—but even more intense. Voices and images and scents and textures rose up from deep inside me. I grabbed my notepad and flipped it open to the first blank sheet.

I couldn't write fast enough. I remembered conversations with Mom, games I'd played with my sisters, boat rides with Dad. I wrote down funny things and sad things, dialogue and description. That could be a story, I found myself thinking as I scribbled notes about the time I stole a pie Mom had just baked for a party and Noelle and I ate the whole thing and then got in huge trouble, or that, or that . . .

Later, back at home, I read over the things I'd written. Then I put my mechanical pencil to a clean sheet of narrow-ruled paper. I wrote five pages without stopping: a story in the form of an imagined conversation between me and my great-grandmother Flora Elizabeth White.

I knew it was good even before I turned it in on Tuesday. I guess that's how it is when you find your writer's voice—it's like coming home after a long trip and unpacking your suitcase and finally getting to sleep in your own bed again. Everything feels comfortable and effortless.

When Mrs. Cobb returned the story to me during class on Thursday, she gave me a warm smile. "I've been waiting for this, Lily," she said. "Thanks."

I glanced at her comments on the last page. *"Original . . . moving . . . insightful. Would you read this aloud for the group?"*

I looked up. Mrs. Cobb was sitting on the edge of her desk. "We need some volunteers to read this morning." She met my eye. "Lily?"

I hadn't read aloud yet this semester, and as I walked up to the podium I remembered the first time I'd read *last* semester, how nervous I'd been and how I'd salvaged a near-disastrous moment by turning what I'd intended as a serious, if lame, story into a joke. That had been the beginning of my long-running, one-woman show. Today I knew I could count on Mickey's approval. As for the rest of the class . . . This time they can laugh if they want, I thought. I don't care if they like it. I don't care if they like *me*. I like the story, and that's what matters.

But as I cleared my throat and got ready to read, I realized that I *did* care about one person's opinion. My eyes darted to the second desk from the left in the third row. What would Daniel think?

"Um, before I start," I said to my classmates, "I just want to say that the character of Flora in the story is a real person—my great-grandmother, in fact, and she died before I was born, but I feel as if I know her because I have some of her old diaries. So I didn't make her up, but I made up the situation, obviously. Okay." I took a deep breath. "Here goes. This is called 'An Apple Tree for Eleanor.'"

I read my story, about a chance meeting in the orchard between the narrator—me—and sixteen-year-old Flora White, who was distraught over her sister's illness. Together Flora and I talked about our experiences and plotted ways to make Eleanor well again. The story was open-ended; in the last sentence I described myself watching Flora and Eleanor walk off through the misty grove of trees, their arms linked, their long skirts swishing against the dewy grass, and disappear back into the past. The story was upbeat, though. You didn't know if Eleanor would be cured or not, but the possibility was there. The important thing was the connection: between the sisters, between the present and the past. The important thing was hope.

When I finished reading, I lowered my stapled notebook pages and looked shyly up at the class.

Mickey started spontaneously clapping, and a bunch of other people joined in. Daniel smiled—just for a second, and then he made his expression neutral again, but a second was long enough. I clutched my story to my chest and, my heart soaring, went back to my desk. "I really, really liked that," Mickey whispered, giving my bicep a congratulatory squeeze.

I smiled at her, and I smiled at Mrs. Cobb writing about metaphor and simile on the blackboard, and I smiled at the back of Daniel's head. It felt amazingly good, having shared a story that expressed my true feelings and dreams. And it turned out that after all my struggling, it was easy to be myself. I didn't have to put on an act to impress people or wear a costume to get attention. Although I'll always love dressing up, I thought, glancing down at my bandanna print skirt and cowboy boots.

Maybe I'd be dressed in black again tomorrow. Who knew? That was the fun of it.

A couple of other kids in the class read stories, and then we did some writing exercises, and then the bell rang. Mickey hooked her arm through mine, like Flora and Eleanor, and we walked to the cafeteria together.

That Friday, Carlos drove up from Tufts. Laurel and I went to the Village Market to buy stuff for a special dinner.

"Lily," she said as I inspected a melon, "I have to tell you something. Mom and I have talked about it, and I think I'm going to register for the spring term at school."

"That's really great," I told her. Then when I realized what she was saying, I asked, "You're leaving me?"

"Oh, Lily," Laurel replied. "You know I'll always be there if you need me. But I really need to get back to school. Being away from it made me realize I miss it—and how committed I am to the prevet program."

I nodded, even though I still felt kind of sad. "I'm glad, Laurel. You *have* to be a veterinarian. It's what you were born to do."

Laurel smiled, her cheeks pink with pleasure. "You think so?"

"Definitely."

We tossed a shrink-wrapped package of chicken in the cart, and a bag of rice, and some vegetables. We hit the ice-cream aisle, too.

We paid for the food and headed back out to the car. "I bet Carlos is glad you're going back to school, huh?" I asked.

"Yep," Laurel answered as she turned the key in the ignition. "He's really focused on the future, you know? So he was bummed out about me taking time off. He thought my whole college career was going to be derailed. Now, though, I think he really understands why it's important for me to do what I'm doing. And look what's happening, you know? This looks like a turning point for me."

I sighed. "You and Carlos are so intense."

Laurel laughed. "Is that good or bad?"

"It's good," I assured her as we drove south on the Old Boston Post Road. "You're so involved with each other. So committed."

"Well, yeah," Laurel said. "That's what it means to be in a relationship."

I thought about Seth. Obviously he hadn't ended up feeling too committed to me, or me to him.

Turning onto Main Street, Laurel glanced at me out of the corner of her eye. "Whatever happened with Daniel?"

"Nothing," I said with another sigh. "I stayed with Seth, remember?"

"But you and Seth aren't together anymore. Are you still interested in Daniel?"

"I think about him a lot," I admitted. "He's in the writing class. But I really hurt his feelings. I don't know." I shrugged. "Maybe it's better not to have a boyfriend right now. I'm finally figuring out some stuff about myself. I'm building a closer relationship with Mom. That's enough."

"Yeah, but if you really like Daniel . . ."

"I didn't say I really like Daniel," I argued, but I couldn't help picturing that thundery day on the couch at his house, the way I'd leaned over him to give him a kiss. A pretty hot kiss at that. "Okay, I do really like him. But he won't even talk to me."

"Does he still work at Harbor Light Books?" Laurel asked.

"I think so. On weekends."

"There's this book I really want for my birthday," she said, flashing me a smile. "I'll write down the title. You should probably buy it tomorrow because it's a best-seller and that way you'll make sure to get a copy."

So that's how I came to be in the bookstore on Saturday during my lunch hour. Mr. Ballard was behind the counter; Daniel was arranging a new display in the front window. "Hi," I said to him.

Daniel looked up. When he saw it was me, he blushed a little, which I took as an encouraging sign. He wouldn't blush if he didn't care, I thought hopefully. "Hi," he replied.

"So, um, I'm looking for a birthday gift for my sister." I read the title off the scrap of paper Laurel had given me. "Do you have it?"

"Sure. Over here."

I followed him back to a shelf labeled New Hardcover Nonfiction. He pointed to a volume in a glossy cover. "There you go."

I lifted the book down, weighing it in my hand. "Thanks."

"Sure."

I expected him to sprint up to the front of the store again. He didn't, though, so I took that as another encouraging sign and forged ahead. "Um, Daniel. Do you think we could, uh, if you haven't taken a lunch break yet, maybe, er . . ."

Daniel made a big show of checking his watch. "Yeah, I'm about due for a break," he said casually. "I wouldn't mind grabbing a bite to eat."

"Great," I said.

Daniel put my book behind the counter so I could pay for it later, and we walked outside. It was a blustery fall day; the wind whisked leaves along the sidewalk and whipped my long hair into a tangle. "Patsy's?" Daniel asked, pointing up the block.

Did he remember that was where we had our first writing partners date? I hoped so. "Perfect," I replied.

Patsy's wasn't crowded—no place in Hawk Harbor is after Labor Day. We could have sat pretty much anywhere, but without consulting about it we gravitated to a corner booth. Another good sign, I thought. He wants privacy as much as I do.

When we'd ordered our food—a turkey club for me, fish-and-chips for him—I said conversationally, "How do you like Mrs. Cobb's class this year?"

This got the ball rolling. We talked about the project Mrs. Cobb had assigned—to research and write a piece of historical fiction—and argued about whether anyone in the class had done a decent job with the poetry assignment, and debated the virtues of doing anonymous written critiques of our classmates' work instead of having one-on-one writing partners as we'd done in the spring.

Our food came, but we were too busy talking to eat. "Back to the historical fiction thing," I said. "I'm going to use my great-grandmother's diaries and then do some additional research about town history and stuff. Do you think that's kind of cheating, you know, because the diaries aren't really history?"

"They are history," Daniel replied. "Totally. A first-person account. You should definitely work with them and write more stories as good as that other one."

I blushed happily. "You thought that was good?"

"It was great."

We were quiet for a minute. Daniel fiddled with his fork, not quite meeting my eyes. Talking about Mrs. Cobb's class is one thing, I realized. We still have a long way to go on some other topics.

And it was up to me to make the first move. "Daniel, I'm sorry," I said. "I blew it over the summer. I was feeling really scared and confused and dependent on Seth. I wish I hadn't hurt your feelings. I wish I'd known myself better then."

Now he did look up at me, in that incredibly direct way he has. "Why? What would you have done differently?"

"Well . . . that night we met at the Corner Ice Cream Shoppe," I said. "Our walk was pretty . . . short. I would have taken a much longer one." I kicked his foot a little. "You know what I mean?"

He nudged mine back. "I think so."

We started playing footsie, just like that day on

the couch. Then Daniel slid around the bend in the horseshoe-shaped booth and I inched over, too, until we were sitting next to each other behind the little rack that held the ketchup and the salt-and-pepper shakers. We bumped shoulders in our old way, and then I got the nerve to turn my head to look at him. For a long moment we just stared into each other's eyes, and his eyes were so warm and sweet that I found myself wondering, How could I have ever thought this guy wasn't cute?

Then Daniel kissed me. Fast, and next to my mouth rather than on it. Still, it was a kiss, right there in Patsy's Diner. We'd never gotten around to eating, so we had our lunches wrapped to go and walked back to the bookstore. I was late returning to Potluck, but I figured Laurel would understand.

"You know, I wasn't *really* expecting to kiss and make up when I dropped in for that book," I told Daniel.

He laughed. "Yeah, right."

"Well, why did you forgive me?"

He tipped back his head, looking up at the cloud-swept sky. "Because—and I know this is going to come as a huge surprise, Lily—I *like* you."

"Even after everything?"

Daniel shrugged. "Yeah, even after everything. I figured that sooner or later you'd come to your senses and realize that Seth wasn't right for you and I was."

"Really?"

"No, not really." Daniel glanced at me. "Would you have broken up with him if he hadn't broken up with you first?"

I thought about it. "Eventually."

We both thought this over. Then in front of Harbor Light Books, I stopped and turned to face him. "I didn't know what I wanted back then," I said softly. "I do now."

"Yeah?"

"Yeah."

I stood on tiptoes and kissed Daniel lightly on the lips, right in the middle of Main Street. He turned red. "How am I supposed to go back to work now?"

I giggled. Glancing over my shoulder, I saw Laurel watching us from the window of Potluck—she gave me a thumbs-up sign. "I'll kiss you again after work. Think about *that*."

Fifteen

It was late October—Laurel's nineteenth birthday weekend. Mom tried to talk Rose and Stephen out of driving up from Boston for the party because Rose was eight months pregnant and Mom thought she should stay closer to home. "This *is* home," Rose reminded Mom, laughing, as she and Stephen dumped their bags in the front hall on Friday night. "And this is nothing, Mom. My friend Sophie from childbirth class is flying to Chicago this weekend for a wedding!"

Mom rolled her eyes. "She'll be sorry if she has that baby at thirty-five thousand feet, with a flight attendant acting as midwife."

On Saturday morning Sarah worked my shift at Potluck so I could stay home and help Mom bake a carrot cake with cream cheese frosting for Laurel.

"Tonight's going to be the best birthday party ever," Rose predicted. "I don't even care that I'm not the one getting the gifts."

"Speaking of which, who'll do the decorations?" Mom asked. She looked at Rose and Stephen. "How about you two?"

Rose glanced at Stephen. "Actually, we have

an . . . appointment. Here in town, right after lunch. I'm not sure how long it'll take."

"An appointment?" I said, but Rose didn't volunteer details.

I ambushed her at the door when she was putting on her coat—one of Stephen's, actually, because his coats were all that fit her now. She buttoned it over her front—it looked like she had a basketball under there. "An appointment with whom?" I asked.

Rose looked over her shoulder. When she was certain no one else was around, she whispered, "A realtor."

"A realtor?" I whispered back.

Just then Stephen, Laurel, and Carlos stepped into the hall. "We're late," Stephen said to Rose.

"Tell you about it later," my sister promised, giving me a conspiratorial wink as she sailed out the door.

I'd asked Laurel if I could invite Daniel to her birthday party and she'd said yes. He showed up promptly at six, wearing a tie and carrying a big bouquet of autumn wildflowers. "Think Laurel will like these?" he asked, tugging on the knot in his tie.

"She'll love them," I assured him.

Laurel did love the flowers—she put them in a vase in the center of the table. She also loves Mexican food, so Mom and I had cooked up a feast of her favorites: pico de gallo, tortilla soup, stuffed chilies, and fajitas. When we were all around the table, about to dig in, I looked across at Rose. "So?" I asked.

She raised her eyebrows at me. "So what?"

"Your appointment! Are you going to tell us about it?"

Rose smiled. Actually, she'd been smiling since she and Stephen got back from town half an hour ago—her smile just broadened. "Okay, we do have some news," she began. She caught Stephen's eye, and he nodded. He was grinning, too. "We met with a realtor. You know Mrs. Geisler, with the office on the corner—Maribeth Geisler? Anyway, we—"

Abruptly Rose stopped talking. She frowned, a pained grimace on her face, one hand touching her abdomen. "What's the matter?" Laurel asked.

Rose didn't answer right away. She sat tensely, her breath a little bit ragged. Then she let out a big sigh. "Oof," she said. "I don't know; it's weird. I've been having these fake contraction things, Braxton Hicks, all afternoon, but now they're starting to get worse. It's only been like five minutes since the last one."

She shot a puzzled look at Stephen. His mouth dropped open. "Rose, maybe they're not fake contractions," he said, sounding panicky. "Five minutes apart . . . in childbirth class the teacher said . . . what if this is the real thing?"

"It can't be," she said, "because I'm not due until—"

She stopped speaking, her face contorted. "Rose, can you talk during this contraction?" Mom asked.

Biting her lip hard, Rose shook her head no.

Mom smiled at Stephen. "Then this *is* the real thing," she said. "Why don't you get a few things together while I call the emergency room at the hospital and tell them we're on our way over?"

It was a pretty exciting night. Laurel never got around to opening her presents; the cake sat untouched on the kitchen counter under a glass dome. We all went to the hospital, even Daniel, and after an intense two-hour labor Rose gave birth to a baby girl.

We took turns crowding into the labor-and-delivery room to view this newest member of the family. "Look at her," Mom said happily, holding the swaddled infant so Hal could admire her. "Isn't she precious?"

Stephen was grinning from ear to ear. "I'm a dad," he said. "I'm a dad!"

Carlos hugged Stephen, pounding him heartily on the back. Daniel stepped over to shake Stephen's hand. "I feel like I should be handing out cigars," Hal said.

"How about ordering a pizza instead?" Rose suggested. "I'm starving!"

"Someone else may be ready for a meal, too," Mom observed, handing the baby back to Rose.

The nurse who'd helped deliver the baby stuck her head into the room. "That's right, Rose. Why don't you try nursing her?"

"Oh, right. Okay." Rose waved one hand. "Everybody out!"

We crowded back into the hallway so Rose could have some privacy while she breast-fed her new baby. Later we kissed Rose, Stephen, and the baby good night and went home.

"How soon can we go back in the morning, do you think?" I asked Mom after Daniel took off. "Seven? Eight?"

Mom smiled. "Why don't you see when you wake up? You may sleep later than you think."

I was sure it would be like Christmas, and I'd wake up at the crack of dawn. Instead when I finally lifted my groggy head from the pillow, the clock on my night table said ten-fifteen. "Mom!" I yelled, leaping from the bed and racing out into the hall. "Laurel! Are you guys still here? Did you leave without me?"

I looked down the stairs. Laurel and Carlos were standing at the foot, wearing their jackets. "Throw something on and go with us," Laurel invited.

For the first time in my life I got dressed without even looking at the clothes I was putting on. On my way out the door Carlos gave me a strange look. I glanced down. I was wearing a plaid skirt with a striped top. My tights were purple; my shoes were green. "Oh no," I said. "I'd better change. I want to make a good impression on my niece!"

Laurel laughed. "Come on." She grabbed my arm and dragged me out the door. "Supposedly babies can only see, like, six inches in front of their faces. It doesn't matter what you wear."

This was a relief. I didn't want the baby to think I was crazy or anything. "The baby," I said out loud as we drove to the hospital in Carlos's car—Mom and Hal had already gone over. "Do you think they've decided on a name?"

"We'll find out," Laurel replied.

When we got to Rose's room, she and Stephen were alone with the baby, who was sleeping in a little bassinet on wheels. "Mom and Hal went to the cafeteria for a cup of coffee," Rose explained. "Sit down, you guys."

I pulled my chair close to the sleeping baby. "Does she have a name yet?" I asked.

Rose glanced at Stephen and then back at me and Laurel, smiling. "Yes, she does. Her name is Daisy."

"Daisy," Laurel whispered. She was standing by the bassinet, and now she put out a hand to touch the baby's forehead. A tear trickled down Laurel's cheek. "Daisy," she said again.

"Daisy Margaret Mathias," Rose said. "Margaret after Mom, of course."

"It's beautiful," I said. My own eyes full of tears, I thought about the conversation the three of us had had a few weeks ago in the park. "It *is* the perfect name."

Stephen glanced at Carlos. "What do you say we get a cup of coffee, too, and let the sisters have a minute by themselves?"

Carlos nodded. "Good idea."

The guys left and it was just us three. Make

that four. "I wish so much that Daisy were here to see my baby," Rose said. "But I feel as if giving the baby her name will keep her memory close forever. And I want baby Daisy to take after my sisters." Rose smiled. "All of you."

Just then the baby began to rub her face with her tiny red fists and make funny little squeaks that sounded like a cat meowing. "May I?" Laurel asked.

Rose nodded, and Laurel lifted Daisy up. "She's so small!" Laurel exclaimed.

"Six pounds, fourteen ounces," Rose said. "Not bad for a month early."

Laurel carried Daisy over to Rose's bed. Rose laid the baby on her back across her own lap. I sat on one side of Rose with Laurel on the other, and we all gazed at Daisy. "I still can't believe it," Rose said in an awed tone. "I have a daughter."

"It had to be a girl," I pointed out. "What would we do with a boy in this family?"

We all laughed. Rose lifted Daisy up and held her facing outward. "Take a good look," she instructed the baby. "These are your aunts. Very important people."

"We'll help take care of you," I promised my niece.

"I'll take you bird watching," Laurel said, "and teach you the names of wildflowers."

"I'll tell you stories and take you clothes shopping," I said.

Rose smiled. "She won't lack for attention, that's for sure. She'll be spoiled rotten."

Just then Mom, Hal, Stephen, and Carlos came back into the room. "What do you think of Daisy Margaret?" Mom asked, as if she couldn't tell the answer by the smiles on Laurel's and my faces.

"I think it's the prettiest name in the world for the prettiest baby in the world," I declared.

"Ditto," Laurel said.

"Are you ready for some more good news?" Rose asked. "As if Daisy isn't enough?"

"What could it possibly be?" Mom wondered.

"I started telling you about it last night at the dinner table, right before I went into labor," Rose reminded us. "About meeting with Maribeth Geisler, the realtor."

"Right," Hal said. "What was that all about?"

"Well." Rose paused dramatically. She always does that when she has something important to say—it's her trademark. "Stephen's grandparents left him some money in their will, and we decided we wanted to use it for the down payment on a house in the country, up here near our families." She paused again. "We knew exactly which house we wanted, too. So yesterday we took a look at it with Maribeth, and we made an offer on the spot." Another pause. "The owners came back today with a counteroffer, and Stephen just called Maribeth to tell her we'd accept it."

"Where's the house?" I asked.

Rose was smiling at Mom. Mom smiled back at her, a look of disbelief in her eyes. "Is it the house I think it is?"

Rose nodded.

"The Lilac Inn!" I shouted.

"Our old house!" Laurel exclaimed.

We all started talking at once. "We'll use it on weekends and holidays," Stephen said to Hal, "when we need a break from the city."

"Wait'll you see the apple trees I used to climb," Laurel said to Carlos, "and the old porch swing is still there, isn't it, Rose?"

"We'll have Daisy's christening party out on the lawn in the spring," Rose decided, "and you guys know that whenever you visit, you can have your old bedrooms."

"I can't believe it," Mom said. "I just can't believe it!"

Rose turned to Mom. "It's okay, isn't it? At first I worried that maybe it would feel strange. I wondered if I'd ever be able to stop thinking of it as *your* house."

"I know what you mean. But so much time has passed since it was my home." Mom glanced at Hal, and he took her hand. "We'll probably end up buying a place here in town. And we don't need anything nearly so big. That's a house for a young, growing family."

"Will you come for Christmas dinner, though?" Rose asked. "And help me make the roast beef and bake apple pies?"

Mom smiled. "Of course."

For a minute we were all quiet. I looked at my older sister with her husband at her side, holding her baby in her arms. And not only were they parents, but they'd bought a house! I can't believe Rose is so grown up, I thought. And Laurel's going back to college, and I'm almost seventeen. This time next year I'll be in college, too.

Suddenly I thought of something. "I'm not the baby of the family anymore!" I said. "Isn't that awesome?"

Everybody laughed.

I kissed my niece on her pink button nose. "Thanks, Daisy."

Epilogue

Five weeks later, on the day before Thanksgiving, Rose, Stephen, and baby Daisy drove up to Maine to take possession of their new home. We were all so excited about having the house back in the family, we decided to celebrate Thanksgiving there. We cooked at the apartment and then carted the food over to Lighthouse Road, along with folding chairs and card tables because the old place was still unfurnished.

"I brought some tablecloths and candles," Mom said as we set up the card tables in the dining room. Hands on her hips, she gazed around the room. "Would you look at that wallpaper? Yuck!"

"Let's take a tour before we have dinner," Rose suggested.

"We need a tour?" I asked. "Rose, we used to live here."

She laughed. "Yeah, but if you think *this* wallpaper's gruesome, you should see the rest of the house!"

While Hal, Stephen, and Carlos tossed a football

179

on the front lawn, the Walker women strolled through the old house, exclaiming over the changes. "They fixed the broken banister on the staircase," Mom observed, shifting baby Daisy to her other shoulder.

"They kept the house in pretty good shape," Rose agreed. "It has a new furnace and a new roof. But their taste in interior decoration was dismal."

The owners of the Lilac Inn had been heavily into purple and cherubs. "Look at Laurel's room!" I squealed when we were on the second floor.

Laurel groaned. "Fuchsia with a heart border. Gross."

"Oh, come on," Rose teased. "Isn't it romantic?" She went to the window and pushed up the sash. "Hey, Carlos, get up here!" she shouted. "Wait'll you see Laurel's old bedroom. It's a total make-out palace!"

We went to my old room next. "Wow," Laurel said. "It looks like a bordello."

I put out a hand to touch the wallpaper. It was dark blue and velvety. "I like it," I said. "It's kind of gothic. Would you keep it like this, Rose?"

"Are you kidding?" she hooted. "As soon as Daisy's old enough for one of those baby swings, I'm sticking her in it so I can start stripping wallpaper. This room'll be the first to go."

At the end of the hall we came to the master bedroom. "This is the only room they didn't change," Rose commented as we stepped inside.

"I think the innkeepers must've slept here."

Mom and Dad's old room had tall windows facing out over the apple orchard. The wallpaper was pale blue with tiny white flowers.

We all fell silent. I could picture the room as it had been: Mom and Dad's four-poster bed against the far wall, the big dresser between the two windows, Mom's dressing table and mirror next to the closet, an easy chair with ottoman and floor lamp in the corner. I remembered coming in here on mornings when Dad didn't get up early to go out on the boat. He'd want to sleep late, but I'd bounce on top of him and tickle him. And when I had bad dreams, Mom and Dad would let me sleep in between them. Their big bed had seemed like the safest spot in the whole world.

I looked at Rose. "This will be Stephen's and my room," she said quietly. "I don't plan to change anything about it."

Mom patted the baby on the back. She nodded wordlessly, then turned to step back into the hall.

The innkeepers had updated the bathroom fixtures, which we all agreed was great. While Rose asked Mom's advice about refinishing wood floors, Laurel and I wandered back downstairs. "Do you think it's weird or wonderful?" I asked her.

"Both," she said.

Fifteen minutes later we'd set the card tables and put out the food. Before taking our chairs, we stood at our places, clasping each other's hands with our heads bowed as Stephen said grace. "I know we're all ravenous," he said, "but I want to drag this out a little longer. We all have so much to be thankful for today. Why don't we each say something?"

He looked at Rose. She nodded. "Today and every day, I am thankful for my wonderful family," she said.

Mom smiled at Rose, her eyes sparkling with tears. "I'm so glad to have such a beautiful grand-child." She gave Rose, Laurel, and me a playful look. "I sincerely hope someday to have many more."

"I'm thankful for Rose's recording contract," Laurel put in. "I think my sister is the best singer in the world, and I know she's going to be a big star."

Rose beamed. The contract had come through just the week before. "And I thought I'd never have a career after the baby," she said.

"As for you, Laurel," Stephen put in, "we're psyched that you're going back to school in January."

Laurel smiled. "I've signed up for a tough course load, but every time I start worrying about it, I think about Mom. If she can run a business, I can beat biochemistry!"

Carlos was looking at Laurel. "Are we going to tell them?" he asked her.

She looked back at him, blushing. "You mean now?"

"Sure," he said. "What time could be better?"

Laurel nodded. "You're right." She turned from Carlos to look at Mom. "Mom, I know you're going to think I'm too young, but—"

"You're engaged," Mom said quietly.

Her eyes bright and her cheeks pink, Laurel nodded.

"Oh, sweetheart." Mom crossed to Laurel and clasped both of her hands. "I'm so happy."

Personally, I was so thrilled, I was about to burst.

"Don't worry, Mom," Laurel said as she and Mom embraced. "We're going to wait till after I graduate to get married."

"I think that's a good idea," Mom said.

"Has everyone had a chance to be thankful?" Hal asked.

"Nope, nope," I said. "I'm thankful for a lot, too. For all the same things you guys have mentioned, but a few others as well. I'm thankful that I have the world's greatest boyfriend. . . ." Daniel and I had been a couple for more than a month now, and I was pretty sure we'd be going out forever. "And the world's greatest writing teacher, who came up with the world's greatest idea for a book."

"What book?" Rose asked.

"Tell them about it, Lil," Mom said.

"I'm going to edit Great-grandma Flora's diaries and turn them into a book, with my own reminiscences in there, too," I explained. "It will be a family history of the Walkers over the generations."

"That is the best idea ever," Rose said.

"I'm glad you think so," I said, "because I have to interview all of you for stories to put in the book."

"Okay," Hal said, his eyes twinkling. "*Now* can we eat?"

For a few minutes there was a lot of noise: chairs scraping, platters and bowls being passed, people saying "please" and "thank you." Then the room grew still except for the sound of silverware clinking on china.

When Stephen took his first bite of Mom's stuffing and gravy, he lifted his eyes with a sigh of appreciation. "Now *that's* something to be thankful for," he declared. "This may be an unconventional Thanksgiving in some ways, but Maggie's cooking is as awesome as ever."

Hal had been pouring wine into the glasses— just a drop in mine so I'd have something to toast with. "Here's to many more holiday meals together," he said, lifting his glass.

"Here's to family," Rose said, looking at the baby, who was sleeping in a basket on the floor next to the table.

"Here's to sisters," Laurel said, smiling at me and Rose with her heart in her eyes. We held each other's gaze for a long moment. I have the best sisters in the whole world, I thought.

"And to brothers-in-law," Stephen added with a wink at Carlos.

"Here's to much happiness for Rose and

Stephen and Daisy in their new-old house," Mom said.

"It's everybody's house," Rose said. "I really want us all to spend time here together. That's why we bought it."

Mom turned to me, and we clinked our glasses. "Lily and I will be over here all the time, won't we?"

I pictured myself sitting under an apple tree, writing stories. I'd baby-sit Daisy and take her for stroller walks on summer days. When she got bigger, I'd show her all my great old hiding places. I'd even help strip wallpaper!

I nodded, a big smile on my face. "Definitely," I said. "Welcome home, everyone."

Julie Garwood

A Girl Named Summer

Julie Garwood's tales always sparkle with the magic that comes from falling in love. Now her talent shines brighter than ever in an unforgettable tale about young love meant especially for younger readers.

When it comes to falling in love, the best thing to be is...yourself.

Coming mid-October

From Archway Paperback
Published by Pocket Books

2000